⫴ **W9-AAQ-586**

PLOUGHSHARES

Spring 2010 • Vol. 36, No. 1

GUEST EDITOR
Elizabeth Strout

EDITOR-IN-CHIEF
Ladette Randolph

MANAGING EDITOR
Andrea Drygas

FICTION EDITOR
Margot Livesey

POETRY EDITOR
John Skoyles

FOUNDING EDITOR
DeWitt Henry

FOUNDING PUBLISHER
Peter O'Malley

ADVISORY EDITORS

Sherman Alexie | Russell Banks | Andrea Barrett | Charles Baxter | Ann Beattie | Madison Smartt Bell | Anne Bernays | Frank Bidart | Amy Bloom | Robert Boswell | Henry Bromell | Rosellen Brown | Ron Carlson | James Carroll | David Daniel | Madeline DeFrees | Mark Doty | Rita Dove | Stuart Dybek | Cornelius Eady | Martín Espada | B. H. Fairchild | Carolyn Forché | Richard Ford | George Garrett | Lorrie Goldensohn | Mary Gordon | Jorie Graham | David Gullette | Marilyn Hacker | Donald Hall | Joy Harjo | Kathryn Harrison | Stratis Haviaras | DeWitt Henry | Edward Hirsch | Jane Hirshfield | Tony Hoagland | Alice Hoffman | Fanny Howe | Marie Howe | Gish Jen | Justin Kaplan | Bill Knott | Yusef Komunyakaa | Maxine Kumin | Don Lee | Philip Levine | Margot Livesey | Thomas Lux | Gail Mazur | Campbell McGrath | Heather McHugh | James Alan McPherson | Sue Miller | Lorrie Moore | Paul Muldoon | Antonya Nelson | Jay Neugeboren | Howard Norman | Tim O'Brien | Joyce Peseroff | Carl Phillips | Jayne Anne Phillips | Robert Pinsky | Alberto Ríos | Lloyd Schwartz | Jane Shore | Charles Simic | Gary Soto | Elizabeth Spires | David St. John | Maura Stanton | Gerald Stern | Mark Strand | Christopher Tilghman | Richard Tillinghast | Chase Twichell | Jean Valentine | Fred Viebahn | Ellen Bryant Voigt | Dan Wakefield | Derek Walcott | Rosanna Warren | Alan Williamson | Eleanor Wilner | Tobias Wolff | C. D. Wright | Al Young | Kevin Young

ASSOCIATE EDITORS
Simeon Berry, Kate Flaherty, Maryanne O'Hara

ASSISTANT EDITORS
Akshay Ahuja & Sara Beigle

EDITORIAL ASSISTANT
Lindsay Sainlar

COPYEDITOR
Carol Farash

BLOG EDITOR
Jay Baron Nicorvo

ePUBLISHING CONSULTANT
John Rodzvilla

INTERNS
Stacey Friedberg, Adrienne Chan, Sarah Stetson, Joshua Garstka

READERS

Jana Lee Balish | Sarah Banse | Sean Campbell | Anne Champion | Kirstin Chen | Jenn De Leon | Fabienne Francois | Taylor Gibbs | Christopher Helmuth | Ethan Joella | Eson Kim | Mary Kovaleski | Andrew Ladd | Jason Lapeze | Liz Lee | Nina MacLaughlin | Valerie Maloof | Sage Marsters | Alexandria Marzano-Lesnevich | Autumn McClintock | Leslie McIntyre | Danielle Monroe | Mallory Moore | Nadia Moskop | Casey Nobile | Jennifer Olsen | Linwood Rumney | Matt Salesses | Nick Sansone | Kate Senecal | Ian Singleton | Brooks Sterritt | Katherine Sticca | Julie Story | Angela Voras-Hills | Nico Vreeland | Caitlin Walls

Ploughshares, a journal of new writing, is guest-edited serially by prominent writers who explore different and personal visions, aesthetics, and literary circles. *Ploughshares* is published in April, August, and December at Emerson College, 120 Boylston Street, Boston, MA 02116-4624. Telephone: (617) 824-3757. Web address: pshares.org. Email: pshares@emerson.edu.

Subscriptions (ISSN 0048-4474): $30 for one year (3 issues), $54 for two years (6 issues); $39 a year for institutions. Add $24 a year for international ($10 for Canada).

Upcoming: Fall 2010, a fiction issue edited by Jim Shepard, will appear in August 2010. Winter 2010-11, a poetry and prose issue edited by Terrance Hayes, will appear in December 2010.

Submissions: Starting summer 2010, *Ploughshares* will have a new reading period. The new reading period is from June 1 to January 15 (postmark and online dates). All submissions sent from January 16 to May will be returned unread. Please see page 201 for editorial and submission policies.

Back-issue, classroom-adoption, and bulk orders may be placed directly through *Ploughshares*. Microfilms of back issues may be obtained from University Microfilms. *Ploughshares* is also available as CD-ROM and full-text products from EBSCO, H. W. Wilson, ProQuest, and the Gale Group. Indexed in M.L.A. Bibliography, Humanities International Index, Book Review Index. Full publishers' index is online at pshares.org. The views and opinions expressed in this journal are solely those of the authors. All rights for individual works revert to the authors upon publication. *Ploughshares* receives support from the National Endowment for the Arts and the Massachusetts Cultural Council.

Retail distribution by Ingram Periodicals, Source Interlink, and Ubiquity. Printed in the U.S.A. by The Sheridan Press. Page composition and production by Quale Press.

Elizabeth Strout photo by Miriam Berkley.

CONTENTS

Spring 2010

INTRODUCTION
Elizabeth Strout   7

FICTION
Richard Bausch, *We Belong Together*   9
Lisa Cupolo, *Long Division*   19
Mary Gordon, *Ars Longa*   36
Amy Hempel, *Greed*   53
Carol Keeley, *Cremains*   71
Marjorie Kemper, *A Memo from Your Temp*   88
Scott Nadelson, *Dolph Schayes's Broken Arm*   109
Joyce Carol Oates, *Distance*   125
E. V. Slate, *The Sailor*   142
Kathryn Staley, *Marty*   164

POETRY
Amy Beeder, *After Aristophanes: take a twig*   13
Dan Bellm, *Doorway*   14
Justin Bigos, *Fassbinder*   15
Paula Bohince, *Wishbone*   16
Cathy Smith Bowers, *Defenestrer*   17
    More Weight   18
Ha Kiet Chau, *A Woman's Warfare*   24
    She's My Rainbow   26
Bruce Cohen, *Rummaging*   28
Michael Collier, *At the End of a Ninetieth Summer*   29
Carol V. Davis, *Eating Crow*   31
    Marshland   33
Jehanne Dubrow, *The Crowd in the City Square*   34
Robert Farnsworth, *Archive*   43
    Theatre   45

Stephen Gibson, *Life Study* 47
Doreen Gildroy, *Celestial Room* 48
Bob Hicok, *a bouquet of violence* 49
   Aubade shaped like breasts or arrows 50
   Tree of life 51
Edward Hirsch, *September Song* 58
David Kirby, *Baby Handle* 60
Mark Kraushaar, *Arthur* 63
   The Cat and the Fiddle 65
Dana Levin, *Her Dream* 66
Bridget Lowe, *Anti-Pastoral* 67
   The Pilgrim Is Bridled and Bespectacled 68
   The Pilgrim Looks at the World from Above 69
Jynne Dilling Martin, *Always Throw the First Fish Back Into the Sea* 79
   The Fads and Fashions of our Life and Times 80
Michael Milburn, *Divorcée* 81
James Thomas Miller, *Who Can't Handle Me Is You* 82
Roger Mitchell, *Looking at an Old Photograph* 84
   Mouth 85
Honor Moore, *Overnight at Key West* 86
   Sunblind at Huayapam 87
Amy Newman, *The Cat* 96
   Making Small Talk, the Cashier at the Grocery Store
      Inadvertently Creates a Religion 98
D. Nurkse, *1967* 99
   The Surface 101
Rebecca Okrent, *Gratified Desire* 102
   Star Sapphire 103
Linda Pastan, *Anatomy* 104
   Pastoral 105
   Traveling Light 106
Beth Woodcome Platow, *Marriage, East Berlin* 107
Katha Pollitt, *Angels* 118
Chelsea Rathburn, *Sweet Nothings* 120
Eric Rawson, *Hotel Razing* 122
Jay Rogoff, *Swanilda Meets Her Twin* 123

Nicholas Samaras, *Crashing Slow and Sudden* 124
Austin Segrest, *The Spanish Steps: Keats Departing* 134
Alan Shapiro, *Park Bench* 135
   Stone Church 137
   Bookstore 140
Faith Shearin, *Being Called Ma'am* 155
   Not Knowing 156
   The Old Boyfriends 158
Charlie Smith, *It Gets a Little Hazy About Now* 159
Jeffrey Thomson, *Where Do Your Poems Come From?* 161

ABOUT ELIZABETH STROUT
   A Profile by Ladette Randolph 174

AVOCATION
   A Plan B essay *by Antonya Nelson* 180

BOOKSHELF
                                                 184
Akshay Ahuja reviews *The Geometry of God*, by Uzma Aslam Khan
Fady Joudah reviews *Restoration: Poems*, by Christina Pugh
Michael Morse reviews *The Art of Syntax: Rhythm of Thought, Rhythm of Song*, by Ellen Bryant Voigt
Laura van den Berg reviews *All That Work and Still No Boys*, by Kathryn Ma

EDITORS' SHELF
193

EDITORS' CORNER
194

CONTRIBUTORS' NOTES
195

Cover: Varujan Boghosian, *Emperor of Ice Cream (detail), 2008, (Wallace Stevens' poem)*, mixed media construction, 23 7/8 x 31"
Courtesy Berta Walker Gallery, Provincetown

ELIZABETH STROUT
Introduction

There was something secretive about it.

When I walked into the library and turned right and kept walking, they were there. Had I ever seen a magazine before I got to college? I had. Had I ever seen a literary journal? I had not. I was a seventeen-year-old girl who left high school a year early, not because I was some whiz kid, but because of the unremarkable and simple reason that I hated being there. So I was glad a college accepted me. But those first weeks on campus, I was certain that every person I passed by on the tree-lined quad was much smarter than I was, knew much more about *everything*. Even my class in music intimidated me. The professor was unsmiling. Students raised their hands. They had things to say about Mozart. I kept my head down. When I went into the library, I kept my head down because the place was dotted with confident-looking students, reading in the chairs that overlooked the quad, or sprawled with books in a carrel.

It was on one of those first fraught days that I walked into the library, and immediately turned right so as to get out of sight of anyone who might glance at me and recognize my sense of discomfort. That's when I saw, attached to a stack and sticking out with quiet authority, a sign that stated the lovely word: PERIODICALS. I would go find *The Atlantic,* and *The New Yorker;* their familiarity would comfort me. But I found a whole row of other things. Journals, some thick, others quite thin, lay on a tilting shelf with their faces toward me. Some had colorful covers, some had very simple and unassuming covers. Inside them—the type pressed into the paper, so that even touching them brought a certain thrill—I found story after story, poem after poem. Who knew? I had not known.

That first year in college the discovery of those literary journals seemed like my secret alone. No one seemed to talk about them! And so I didn't either. But I would slip one from the holder and go over by the window and read with hungry happiness.

There were stories of love. A young woman named Sarah was adored by the narrator. They went hiking together. They were intimate. They split up. But he loved her, and she loved him. Still, they split up. I thought about it back in my dorm room. I was deeply affected, and received from it an odd courage, knowing that my own heartbreak would happen someday, as of course it did. People lived through it. I learned something of that by reading that story. I learned from reading the poems that I was not the only one who inwardly groaned at the way sun fell across the snow; I learned that a parent's death caused a terrifying silence.

Of course I could have, and probably did, learn these things from the stories and poems read in my various English classes, or from the books I had read before college. But there was something about that array of literary magazines off to the right in the library that seemed to reach inside me the most. Over the next months and the following years, I learned to recognize the names of some of the writers and poets as they published in one place and then another, and they felt like my friends, even though I had never met them. Abundance is the word I think of now. Such an abundance of life: the tiny and the huge—all there. Waiting.

RICHARD BAUSCH
We Belong Together

Now they were in the car, a half hour late, on the way to lunch with Tina. Mary drove. Mary had said she'd leave him if he lied to her about other women again, and now she was leaving. It had all come out this morning. He felt sick. She seemed calm, determined, cold. It was early spring. The country was crazy with color. Everything blooming, everything lush and fresh, the very air promising renewal and replenishment. The car radio was on low. The only sound. The presidential election had worn into its third year, and the air was full of exaggerated campaign talk, lies, and attacks. Empty promises. Nothing would change; or else it would.

The restaurant where Tina waited was called Belle. It had a glass front and thirties retro décor. Tina was stylish and statuesque, a vegetarian. She had already ordered her salad and was eating it. She had also ordered bread and a half carafe of Sancerre. You could see her in the window of the place. She waved to them and smiled.

Frank got out of the car. All the promise of his twenties and early thirties had played out in a string of compromises. It hurt him that all the people he worked with were on their way elsewhere, believed that better things were ahead. He had told Mary in the beginning that if they had Tina's friendship it could help him get ahead in the agency. Another lie. He wasn't going anywhere in the agency, which sold advertising. More lies. Getting out of the car, he realized that he did not want this change: Mary leaving him, ending things. His gorge rose. He watched her drive down the block. She would have the locks changed on all the doors of home. He looked at Tina in the window with her puzzled expression.

When he stepped through the shadow in the entrance, he saw his own face in the reflection, pale as death. He went into the men's room and washed his face. When he came out, she waved at him again, still looking puzzled. He walked over to her and sat down. "She knows," he said. "She's leaving me."

Tina stared at him.

"I guess it was coming to this."

"Oh, God. That's what's going on."

"This morning," he said. "It's why we were late."

"What she must think of me."

"No," he said. "It's all me. Believe me." And now he experienced a surprising sudden lifting inside. It was almost elation. The thing was here at last, and would settle in its own way, and they would go through it together. They were free. It had just come to him, looking at the soft curve of her neck, that they were free.

She took a sip of the wine. Her hand shook. He said: "I feel like my whole life is a series of broken promises. The whole world: nobody living up to anything and all of it turning to lies, lies, lies, lies, lies." He was very dramatic, controlling the panic. He knew she liked the drama, and found him attractive when he was despairing. But he believed it too, now, and felt it. "I'm—I was so tired of all the lies."

"All those broken promises," she said. "Whose were they?"

"I'm talking about life. And—and happiness."

"But you made promises too."

"What're you getting at?"

"I'm just responding to you, Sweetie. You said broken promises."

"All right. Mine too. My whole life—"

She took a last bite of her salad, and then finished the wine in her glass. She shook her head, setting the glass down soundlessly on the table.

"But all that's done with, now and we're free," he said.

She murmured, "Oh, God, Frank."

"I know," he told her. "But it was always coming to this and we knew that."

"I guess we did."

He poured a little of the wine and drank it down.

"You're so hurt, my darling. Look at you. You're pale as death."

"Let me get a real drink." He signaled the waiter across the room. The waiter knew them from previous visits. He came over. Frank ordered a Scotch, double.

She waved anything else away for her, and sat there looking at him.

"I'm sorry," Frank said. "I'll be fine. This is a good thing. It's what we've wanted for so long. It's freedom."

"You don't sound like you believe it."

"It's not a matter of faith."

She was silent.

"Is it."

Presently the waiter brought his drink. Frank took a long swallow of it. "I guess I thought it would play out a little less—I don't know, less abruptly."

"Abruptly. What an odd word that is. I think that's such an odd word."

"It's a word."

She poured more wine for herself and took a little, gazing at him over the lip of the glass.

He leaned forward, to click his glass against hers. "To freedom."

She said, "Yes, freedom." They touched glasses and drank.

"I love you," he said.

"You sound like someone bringing death news."

"I love you," he said again.

"Maybe this isn't the time to talk like this. You said it was a little sudden for you. I mean abrupt. Sorry."

"It was upsetting. Yes. The way it all just came tumbling out. But it's done."

She reached across the table and took his hand. "I feel awful, honey. But I can't stay here."

He said, "What?"

"I can't. I feel ill."

She did not look ill. Her eyes glittered. He said, "Don't you understand what this means? Mary knows. She's leaving me. It's done. I can come home with you tonight."

"But do *you* hear what you just said?"

He looked down at his hands where they cradled the drink.

"She's leaving *you*."

"But it's—it's what we wanted. What *I* wanted anyway."

"No. You're not listening, Frank."

"What difference does all that make? We're free now."

"When you got out of that car and started in here," she said, "You looked like a man who had just learned he was going to die in the morning. You were scared down to your bones."

He took another long swallow. "Jesus Christ, Tina."

"The look on your face as she drove away."

"Baby," he said. "It was upsetting, sure—"

She interrupted him. "No. You were a man who was realizing something terrible. It was all over you like a—like a light."

The waiter came to ask what he wanted to eat.

"I'm not hungry," he said.

"Put the whiskey on mine," she said. The waiter left with her credit card. The two of them sat there while the others in the place talked and laughed. On the other side of the room, a man sang part of a song to two couples; all of them took it up. They were old friends. Others toasted the pleasant spring weather, agreeing that it had been a long winter. Near the entrance to the restrooms, a waitress dropped a tray with two glasses on it. A man at the nearby table helped her pick it up.

The waiter brought her check. She signed it.

Frank looked out at the street. There were many people going back and forth in the bright sun, and cars stopping and then idling forward. The glass on the storefronts across the way glared at him.

She got up and leaned down and barely brushed his forehead with her cool lips. "Bye, lover. I'll be in touch. I need some time. I think maybe we both need some time."

"What?" he said. "What?"

"I'll call you," she said. "Promise."

After Aristophanes: take a twig

push up the wick, when the dark comes early.
That's marrow dark. Waiting-for-the-savior dark.

Keep spare lamps for when cocoons turn mute:
their prophecy spilled scale & tattered wing.

For when no wasp will overwinter & no beetle.
When that iridescence litters fields

lace tight your goods. Somewhere in the barn
a cache: broken bottle, stolen keys—

no one has looked for them in years, or remembers:
still you can't sleep for the brimstone sweats

recalling every error, every mistranslation.
Suffer the darkness. Or take a twig.

DAN BELLM
Doorway

He goes out the door as someone I don't know.
Not the boy-man I was at 17
but somewhat lagging behind, somewhat further ahead,
dressed carefully for others in red and black,
his body a deliberate mystery.

No idea what he knows, what he says, what he does.
I'm not supposed to know, only the surfaces of fact,
of where he's going, the stated plan, the hour of return.
Left behind with a trail of his belongings
across the hallway floor, the clothes he knew not to wear—

I'm free to pick them up and sort them if I want
or to leave them where they are,
free to raise the window for a little air.
I know enough to stay out of his room,
more than my father did,

I know enough to ask for one quick hug
before he goes, he knows enough to give it,
and what comfort it lends me is this instance
of nakedness I wait for, the oldest illusion there is
not being shed, but overthrown.

JUSTIN BIGOS

Fassbinder

He couldn't wait to finish a film before
he started the next, forty-three total plus
the nine-hundred-thirty-minute TV series;
refused to commit to any one lover,
man or woman; fucked his actors in Munich
hotels and Morocco châteaus; left a trail
of broken hearts, one ex-wife, four wrecked
Lamborghinis, two suicides; popped pills
to stay awake and pills to fall asleep,
coke, booze, you name it; lit one cigarette
off another, ate the worst German
foods, braunschweiger and bratwurst
fried in fat, had to get it all down, squeeze
it all in and keep it up, never enough
time, the work the work was all that mattered
it was never enough, I'm saying
out of breath at 2:47 a.m. to
the woman I want to marry

PAULA BOHINCE

Wishbone

Psychic rib
soaped clean, skeleton
key to every lock
in this house. *Heartless,*
this place, as I've
come to christen it.

The wish then
abandoned in the soap
dish, near the wet
bone china.

Last Christmas saw us
shivering at Lake Erie,
stroking the battered nose
of a dinghy.

Abandoned. Bone-
clean, its hull scoured
with saltwater
for a year.

Don't say it. Pluck
the lyre from the capon's
body and break it.

CATHY SMITH BOWERS
Defenestrer

First you were windowed, then windowless.
Window-rich, then poor. They did it with such
finesse, for a moment you thought to thank them,
the way your graceless limbs with a dancer's grace
made art of the artless air. Nothing original here.
Think of those two whose flailings shattered sky.
Who later praised the benevolent courtyard dung
that safely delivered them. And should they, too,
count? Those not thrown, with no other recourse
than to jump? Strange hands of strangers strangely
clasped as earth leapt up to welcome them?

      poor   windowless   moment.
did they First? were? Window-rich, you
    thought,   then   then   with   such
               finesse
    a *thank you*   to them   for it,
the way   of that artless air   your graceless limbs
    with a   dancer's grace   made art.
  Think   praised   original   sky,
those who safely   delivered Nothing
   of   the benevolent two
whose   courtyard   flailings
   later   shattered   dung.
  They
     too
      leapt.
        recourse with of should?
them windowed here   Strange jump
      hands up not to,
as to Those   welcome   other
than   the   thrown.
  And strangely earth
      no strangers,
  count them,
    clasped.

CATHY SMITH BOWERS
More Weight

They'd take her child away, unless he shed more weight.
But every time he cried, she fed. More weight.

My little niece too light, and snow not dense enough,
I squeezed myself behind her on the sled: more weight.

So thin her body cannot warm itself, she picks at the meager
salad on her plate. Her greatest dread—more weight.

How many have passed through courts that never proved
their guilt? Yet all still now quite dead. More wait.

One stone on old Giles Cory's chest. Another. Then a next.
Confess, confess! the crowd cried out. But all he said: *More weight.*

Drunk nights. Hunger. Mother, father, two brothers dead. The bridge.
Pray, Cathy, someone said. She did. More weight.

LISA CUPOLO
Long Division

Kenya, Africa. Africa! Nine thousand miles from Portland. My wayward son Tim walks toward me with four tall, dark-as-midnight women. He has seen me, I'm quite sure of it, but nothing about his gait changes. He arrives at the tent and doesn't say a word, or make any motion toward me. The thirty or so Kenyan women standing around are curious, and openly gawking. Tim indicates what he wants people to do, setting up two wobbly card tables under the shade of the tent and getting them to form two lines. I walk over to him.

"Hello," he says.

"I can't believe I've tracked you down." I hold my arms out for a hug. We manage it, but it's awkward. I pull away before tears come. I don't think he noticed.

"Well, I'm happy to see you," he tells me, as I say again, "I've finally tracked you down."

Then I'm just standing there watching him do the work of organizing things in this camp, or whatever it is. When he was little I helped him with math problems once. Once. His mother talked about that a lot in the weeks before she died; the only instance of my being a father to him. The famous instance. So much bitterness. He was always so much his mother's boy, and he all but raised his sister. Maddy. It's Maddy I've come to see him about.

Arriving in this country last week was like stepping off an elevator into hell. When I was much younger, I was hungry for travel, for looking at things. But never Africa. Not ever once.

When he pauses to drink from his canteen I say, "I'm here to ask you to come home."

He shakes his head, swallowing. "I thought for a second you were here to help. It's a perfectly ridiculous thought, I know." He makes his way over to a chair under an acacia, and I follow him. There is a line of twenty women and they seem relieved when he sits down and they sit around at his feet like kids at a story reading.

"It's your sister," I tell him. "She's gone into one of her unreachable places again. I thought if she could see you. Just for a visit."

"Not possible, Dad," Tim says. "How did you track me down, as you put it?"

"I hired someone who does that for a living."

"You wasted more money."

He motions for the first woman to come up. She has a baby with her, a tiny thing who is nursing, though the woman looks way beyond childbearing years. Tim greets her warmly. There is little space between them and I feel like an intruder, but I don't move back.

"I walk five kilometers," she tells him, "then I wait an hour for the bus before I reach my workplace. There are four nurses, but I am alone on duty and look after around seventy to one hundred, mostly HIV patients."

"There aren't others who can relieve you?" Tim says.

"They are too afraid of infection. Many times the next nurse doesn't show up, so I am working twenty-four hours." The woman's face doesn't change while she talks. Her expression isn't exactly detached, yet there's very little feeling in it. She's just telling facts, like someone cataloging crimes.

"I'm so sorry," Tim says. He gives her his bottle of water. "You have to take a meal?"

"My husband is furious." Her swollen eyes look down at the brown earth.

Tim stands up. He hands her pieces of paper, coupons of some sort.

"I am here for the other women," she says.

He leads her to a group sitting on a small patch of grass. They wear brightly colored yet faded patterned cloth, some worn as skirts and others tied loose at the back of the neck. Their heads are covered in scarves. They are beautiful women from a distance. Up close their teeth are yellow and rotting and lines crease their faces. A few of them are laughing, but to me it sounds nervous, stressed. I go over to them and their expressions turn vinegary.

"How are you, Mzungu, father of Tim?" one of them says. Mzungu means white man. I should've known.

When I ask them about themselves they are guarded: God is good to them, they say, they are glad to see me. I'm amazed at how clear and unaccented their English is.

"How are you? How are you?" I say, nodding, but I don't really want to know the answer. I pretend I am walking over to a frangipani tree but I slow down.

"I have eight grandchildren between two and fourteen that are with me. I have six children of my own and four are dead. One of my sons is now very sick and, God willing, he will be well. My husband left us a long time ago. I believe he's still alive."

I realize, my God, they're swapping stories. They're sitting in a circle now and each one takes the others through her own corner of hell.

My son is like the camp counselor in a camp you've never seen the likes of—walking around with his clipboard and his preppy shorts, and the wide hat with the loose string down his chest. Any second, I expect that he'll pull a whistle from his pocket and blow it. He's making small speeches to various groups, a few are weaving baskets, and over to one side there's an outdoor cooker where four women stand over two large metal pots. Steam rises above their heads. I realize that I'm seeing Tim as he is in the world, with no reference to me at all. I'm a businessman, even in retirement. Tim is all pathos. I have always believed that you have to pay close attention to what the other guy is thinking; Tim just anticipates what others might need.

"You're the only one who can do this," I say to him about Maddy. We're eating cassava and ugali. The young woman described it and handed it to me proudly. We're sitting on the hard earth next to a large uneven tree stump, and it's steeply uncomfortable for me. "She needs you. You've always been there for her—you've always been the one who could reach her."

Tim has been more of a parent to Maddy than I ever have, and this is between us, now, but he isn't looking at me. His reaction is like those of the Africans I met in Nairobi; he's letting me do all the talking.

"She's been depressed before," he says. "She's good at getting herself out of these funks."

"She says you've abandoned us."

"She should wake up a little, get out of that bubble of hers." It's strange: here he is, saying the very thing I've always said to him about her. The very thing he would profess to hate about my way of looking at things.

It's pretty clear that Tim's mind is elsewhere; he hasn't even noticed the change in him. "What we're trying to do first," he says, "is make these women understand that they don't have to accept the life they've been handed." He takes a handful of ugali and puts it between his teeth. "We're trying to show them," he goes on, chewing, "that they can choose a different way. They can come to the center and make things and be part of a community."

"I know what you think of me," I say. I hadn't known I would say it. But he goes on. "It's like a witness protection plan without the protection. The witnesses are taught to stand up for themselves."

"Catherine is with her." His ex. I say it to get a rise out of him. "She and Maddy are great pals. Until Maddy started living between the bathroom and the kitchen."

"Does Catherine need money—is that it?"

"What the hell does that say about your sister?"

"No—it's what I'm saying about Catherine."

After a pause, he adds: "Maddy's a grown up. She can handle herself. She knows I love her."

"Man, she won't talk to me. Hasn't done so—and you know this— since your mother and I—and then your mother—that's the thing. I want to get past it. How many times do I have to say, I take the blame for everything. I came all this way, Tim. I found you. I want to make up for it all."

"You're not listening to me," he says. "They're all dying, here, Pops. One after another after another. A full third of the population."

"I know. This would just be for a couple of weeks. One week. You could settle her a little, bring her out of it. She's always responded to you." He's barely listening. It's like he almost finds Maddy's situation, and me, for that matter, annoying.

He starts talking to people at the table, away from me. "I tell them, you know, stick together. I tell them they don't have to have intercourse with their husbands, like the culture says they do. I tell them to go and stay with a friend, run away. We're working on building a safe place for them." He looks back at me. "They believe there's only one way."

"Your sister needs to hear from you. You know that."

"I've got this to do, here."

It comes to me that in his mind I am less father than outsider. "Listen," I say. "You're a better man than me, son. You are. You were always the one she turned to."

He just stares.

"Just one week and I'll send you right back here. First class."

He gazes ahead to the edge of the hill where the women are walking together.

"Please, son."

And then he starts laughing. He fights it, putting a hand over his mouth. "You came all this way. You—all those miles. Did you think you could just collect me like some lost little kid? Maddy's fine. Maddy's indulging herself. She's got her bedroom and her acting and her friendship with Catherine, and I've got the African continent. You found me—now go and find her."

"One week," I say.

Later, he's hugging people, thanking them and packing up his supplies in a small Renault hatchback. Heading off, the savior. I catch myself calculating how much money I should leave for him. I catch myself, again, thinking about money.

One week. That was all I asked of him.

HA KIET CHAU
A Woman's Warfare

Hanoi streets on their last demise do not shine like yellow bananas.
The color of brown spotted ripe bananas for straight eleven eves,
Coated with layers of night fumes.
Seven women on their bicycles steer by a smoggy sundown.
Threatening bombs like alarm clocks tick in my ears,
As war fumes snatch the pretty red ao dai dresses off these women's hips,
Rape their static, numb corpses set for tomorrow's entombment.
Counting the eleven minutes like the one hundred and one
Diminutive black sheep who will never sleep,
They foreshadow deaths between exhausted yawns.

This chest that belongs to me leaps higher
Than the string of soldiers evading gunshots up and down,
Firing along mucky war fields.
This vision that belongs to me is stolen,
Like communist dictators seizing our possessions,
Imprisoning our men until we are penniless,
A black vacuum of nothingness.
Wives wail giving birth on polluted street corners.
A terribly violent penetration precedes,
Rings like panic sirens north and south, up and down,
East and west, through the surrendering city of Haiphong.
Women risk their lives under plunging bombs,
Bemoaning on bended knees for their dying lovers,
As screaming bare babies crash down with fractured skulls.

Death wakes her up in an early mourning,
As men's tongues hemorrhage red blood and spew yellow vomit,
Permeating the demised streets.
A naked offspring bawls like a burnt black cat
Crying for milk when milk is not visible.

This 1972 Vietnamization aftermath,
The bloodshot eyes, so soggy, so sightless.
Sidewalks of a murdered Hanoi, ruined mounds of black mountains
Barring women from ever climbing to the top.
Death tugs my hand, heaves me closer to a light.
Death fights for the fast pulse on my wrist,
For the eight-month fetus in my belly.
Our bodies run for a nearby underground tunnel, our single escape.
We hide like timorous red crabs under protective shells,
As mature men beg for a mercy they rightfully deserve,
For a more lenient peace.

HA KIET CHAU
She's My Rainbow

Is it too soon to murmur in her ear that I miss someone?
The statue of liberty stands so still underneath a rainbow.
She won't mind if I play with the copper flame on her green torch.
She can fool around with my liberated heart until it burns into ashes.
Let me be the one to walk quietly through her meditation.
She's my rainbow after the sun kisses the rain good morning.

Is it too careless to murmur in her ear that I miss someone?
I saw a chocolate spider lounging on liberty's shoulder once.
Never forgot how her colors can lift my moods so effortlessly.
So charmed by her bright webs glistening across a rainbow arch.
Diamond dewdrops hang like silver streamers from the wet sky,
Full of cherry red and berry blue curves.
Minutes shift speechlessly, hours delay dramatically.
Space closes in seconds.
Won't she be my saving grace, my Charlotte, my wisdom?
She can't mumble a word to justify my raw emotions.

Is it too risky to murmur in her ear that I miss someone?
She's my rainbow before the caged sun yawns and the free rain sleeps.
If I asked humbly, would she crave the hourglass of my waist?
I am a brave honeybee tangled inside her alluring web of mystery.
My pink drizzle takes her by storm,
Bathes her in a shower, dresses her in time for supper.
I wish she'd drum on my glass windows with her eight spider legs.
Dare me to come out and play; an hour or two.

Is it too late to whisper in her ear that I miss someone—
And that someone is her?
If I fling my heart into the depths of the cosmic universe,

Will she catch it instantaneously before the earth explodes?
Drop my heart delicately; drop it roughly like rainwater.
But vow to never ever, ever let it smash into those weeping willow trees.
Let my heartbeats dry, let it thump-thump under the mango sun.
She's my rainbow after the sun kisses the rain good morning.

Rummaging

Here is the paint-by-numbers painting of Sitting Bull's pony she painted.
Here is her imitation Navajo loom she used to weave turquoise blankets.
Here is her afternoon martini shaker and the prescription Black Beauties.
Mahjong tiles click rhythmically by arthritic hands of her bilingual generation.

Outside the rain rains sideways, horizontal as this world is, forcing umbrellas
Inside out, causing even the sun to go insane. The rush-hour train stops
At every unpronounceable station; there's no express to her town anymore;
Her beauty parlor hair no longer appears regularly, clogging the shower drain.

Seasons have turned profoundly unseasonal, commercials for funeral homes
Hum effluvium as white background noise; when you need one it's a quick
Flip through the yellow pages with a kind of all-you-can-eat attitude,
A connect-the-dots Dadaism. The dial on the radio circles counterclockwise,

Continuously, stuck on a station from the big band era, squeaky pitched
Static only dogs hear. How hard it is to follow her life's bouncing ball
Out the asylum's third story, ignoring her most personal curfews, escaping
On trains one hears but never sees, diaries composed in disappearing ink.

MICHAEL COLLIER

At the End of a Ninetieth Summer

They drink their cocktails in the calm manner
of their middle years, while the dim lights
around the swimming pool make shadows
of that world they've almost fully entered.

Like Yeats' wild swans their uneven number
suggests at least one of them is no longer mated.
Added up, their several ages are short of a millennium.
This means the melting ice cubes are silent music beneath

their slow talk, and slow talk is how gods murmur
when eternity comes to an end.
The way it feels for these friends who amaze themselves
with what they remember—not the small details—

but how long ago lives happened and how fast.
Occasionally, usually from the wives, there's mention
of the War, as if they'd endured before waiting like this,
except now there's no uncertain homecoming,

no life to be beginning and nothing to complete
that doesn't wear already the aura of completion.
Listen, they are laughing. One eases himself up
to refill his drink. His wife, in a wheelchair, wants one too.

Another makes a joke about making it a double
and gets up to help. They are gone so long,
or not long enough, that someone asks,
"Where's Bob and Jim?"

Now and then a tentacle of the robot vacuum
submerged in the pool breaches the surface,
squirts a welcome spray of water,
then retracts where it continues its random sweeps,

until it breaks into the air again.
Bob and Jim are back, the drinks get passed,
even so Jim's wife asks, "Where did you go?"
Instead of answering, he raises his glass.

CAROL V. DAVIS

Eating Crow

Sing a song of sixpence a pocket full of rye,
Four and twenty blackbirds baked in a pie.
When the pie was opened the birds began to sing,

On TV the *Bizarre Foods* host leans over
a rickety market stall in Bangkok.
He picks at the toothpick bones of a sparrow,
licks his lips and reaches for a second bird,
its skeleton the size of his palm.

A cook to a medieval knight would place
live birds inside a pastry crust.
A great joke, though the real pie was served
after the birds had been released.

Is that how we got the four and twenty blackbirds
whose heads pop through a blanket of pie crust?
Beaks wide to sing their hearts out,
though they are cooked through and through.

In the Middle Ages peafowl was served
on any table worth its weight.
The birds decked out in a mantle of herbs,
green as a king's velvet collar.

The steer's head displayed like
crown jewels on the butcher table
put me off meat that year in Russia,
but no more than the intestines
ladled into a pond of broth.

I may succumb to the occasional hamburger.
Still I wanted to rescue those little birds
from their pinched cages before
they met their deaths in a bath of oil.
To take the fingers of the food show host,
smack them away, before he licked them clean.

CAROL V. DAVIS
Marshland

We are all intruders here
        though we fool ourselves this late winter day,
carving a place on the banks
            to anchor our heels.
We stretch over the water, hoping
        to slip onto the wings of a Great Blue Heron
but afraid to get caught in the trap of reeds, twisting
            in the foul water.
The marsh ignites: will-o'-wisps,
           sprites, a wisp of flames,
torches held aloft by villagers
           marching on the manor.
We've read too many fairytales
           but this much is true:
I heard voices.
           Not the call of a willet or clapper rail
but a child caught beneath the ceiling of water
           the thin reed of its voice
rising in the brackish light.

JEHANNE DUBROW

The Crowd in the City Square

has become one knotted rope
one breath of cabbage soup.

one foot on the cobblestone—
a thousand banners—no—one

flag flapping its red letters
into a satin tatter

because this is the century
of slivers and scraps—beauty

of the dustbin—the crowd knows
that nothing good can follow

from that other prettiness
—the slick summer palaces

of the tyrant—the mansions
iced like cakes for spoiled children—

the crowd wears a glove with holes
in the fingertips and pulls

at the thread—the crowd loses
all feeling in its thin nose—

so lovely to be shattered
not far from the granite stairs

and the tinkling chandelier
in the city of nowhere—

the city of discarded
ironies—lost shoes and scarves

Ars Longa

Here in this little town in Pennsylvania where I spend half the week and the whole long summer, we are urged to buy local. This is a pleasure, not a duty or a difficulty. The rewards are multiple: sticking it to the multinationals, high quality merchandise, real personal exchanges. Becoming known.

The place in town where I am best known is a local fruit and vegetable—well, to call it a store would be far too aggrandizing; it is, after all, only a wooden shack that looks like it might be blown over in a bad storm. It abuts a makeshift greenhouse on one side and on the other an old wagon where you choose your ears of August corn. It is owned and run by Rick and his mother.

I would guess Rick is firmly embedded in his fifties, although I'm not sure at which end of the decade he resides. Approaching sixty, I assume he's younger than I, but I find it difficult to fix a number to our age difference. He's always tan, his face is free of wrinkles, and his hair is a golden blond, but he has the gut and thick, bowed shoulders of a man no longer young, and when, on warm days, his shirt is unbuttoned, there is revealed an effulgence of thick chest hair: silver gray.

His mother, Lorraine, reminds me of a particular kind of shaggy terrier: hyperalert, exceedingly informed, nearly universally ill-pleased. Her wardrobe consists of an impressive array of brightly colored, floral-printed Bermuda shorts, complemented by equally brightly colored T-shirts and several pairs of Technicolor Crocs: indigo, flamingo, lemon lime. It only now occurs to me, writing the words *lemon lime,* that she dresses in response to her merchandise, that the colors aren't in fact indigo and flamingo but blueberry, cherry, tomato, cantaloupe.

When Rick isn't around, Lorraine enjoys making vaguely sexual jokes relying on the theme of fruit. With the occasional reference to the cucumber or banana. She is harder hearted than her son; once when I dropped a cantaloupe she said, "You picked it, it's yours." Rick would never have made me pay for a damaged cantaloupe. She never, as he does, includes an extra ear of corn.

The stand is open from Easter through Christmas. I asked him once what he did in the intervening months.

"Who knows?" he snorted.

I refrained from telling him that he probably did know, that he certainly knew what he had done in the past years, and that the way he posed the question—who knows—is particularly in-apposite, if not a radical definition of a rhetorical statement: because who would know if not he.

I don't know why I had the impulse to press the point, suggesting that perhaps he and his mother traveled south to recover from the hyperbusy spring and summer months. Florida, I offered. Arizona.

"You gotta be kidding," he said. "I'm barely keeping my head above water, without turning into one of them snowbirds."

Rick is a dab hand at picking a perfectly ripe melon. "Just leave this baby on the counter and in two days, lunch time if you want, or supper, but not breakfast, I guarantee it, you'll be pleased." Once I was holding honeydew up to my ear, shaking it for evidence of loose seeds, therefore ripeness. He grabbed the melon out of my hand with ill-concealed impatience.

"You're holding it wrong," he said. "You got to hold it the long way."

Since, to my eye, honeydew is round, I had no idea what he might mean by "the long way."

"From now on, I'll let you do the picking for me. I'll leave it to you," I said. He seemed quite pleased.

But if the impending ripeness of good fruit gave him moments of temporary hopefulness, this was, by a long chalk, the exception. Rick is not one of nature's optimists. The range of his dismay takes in a wide variety of categories, from politics and the economy to the weather and the fate of the planet. Any of these can lead seamlessly to the rising cost of fruits and vegetables and their declining quality.

Every succulent piece of fruit is an exception and no large conclusions can be drawn from it. The arrival of a snowy cauliflower occasions laments about the recent woody broccoli. Late in July, when the first tomatoes were arriving, he said: "Get 'em while you can. I hear there's blight, a virus attacking tomatoes this year. In a couple of weeks every tomato you cut into will show you nothing but hard black stone."

There was no point telling him that the tomatoes in my own unimpressive garden were doing very well, better than they had in many years, as far back as I could remember. He would have snorted derisively. "Just you wait" is what he would have said. It was what he nearly always said upon hearing good news.

The lives of domestic pets were for Rick a particular sign of an unloving universe. He had a real reason for this particular brand of pessimism (I suppose all his dark perceptions had a root in some piece of real history): He had a lovely dog, a Shepherd mix, who always lay peacefully in the parking lot, greeting only those customers whom she could see wished to be greeted by her. One day, the dog was struck with kidney failure and in a week she was dead.

I asked Rick if he considered getting another dog.

"Nah, they just break your heart," he said. "A friend of mine found a mother cat and a litter of kittens, tried to get me to take one. I said no way, but I gave him some money to get the mother spayed. All I could see was hundreds of kittens starving to death."

"But if you'd taken one of the kittens," I said, "you might have enjoyed having it."

"No way," he said, "they just break your heart."

In the same way that Rick could draw convincing strong connecting dots between politics, the economy, and the price of peaches, he was able to join his sad stories of the fates of animals into a larger picture of human perfidy. The friend whom he gave the money to in order to get the mother cat spayed took it and lost it at the OTB.

"And just to show you," he said one day, "when I was really low about losing my dog, my old girlfriend calls me out of the blue to tell me how sorry she is. I wasn't falling for that trap. I know what she thought: she'd get me at a weak moment when I was vulnerable. Well, I've been around the block a few times too many for that one let me tell you. I'm just a little bit too smart for that kind of trick."

I know that Rick likes me, or I think he likes me, and I believe he knows how much I like him, but his commentary on my life is not always complimentary. He asked me why I couldn't support myself by writing, why I needed to teach. Couldn't I write the kind of books that people, "and I mean a lot of people, not just pointy heads" really want to read? He said that if I did that, and I didn't have to teach, I wouldn't have to go back and forth to the city, I could spend all my time in the country. When I told him that I liked combining writing and teaching and that I liked splitting my time between the city and the country, he put an extra ear of corn in my bag, and snorted, "I guess it takes all kinds." When I told him I had to go back to work after Labor Day, he asked:

"Hubby stayin' around up here?"

"Yes, I'll be back on the weekends."

"I guess you're the cash cow."

"Well Rick," I said, like the good wife I want him to believe I am, "it's not quite like that. My husband's retired. He worked for forty-five years."

But I could see Rick wasn't listening. He had his own fish to fry.

"I could never live off a woman. Some of my buddies can, but I can't. It's bad enough when women want to use me for sex. I say, hey, I'm not a sex toy."

I assumed he was kidding. "I have to say, I never thought of you like that, Rick."

The disappointment in his eyes made me feel like a felon. I vowed never to make such a mistake again. I like Rick very much. I want him to be happy.

Today when I pull into the parking lot, he springs out of the door like a jack-in-the-box.

"I was hoping you'd come in today," he says. "I got something I really want to show you."

He picks up what I understand is a framed poem.

"A lady comes in here last week. She rented a house, right on your road, just for a week, just to write poetry, she said. I mentioned your name. She never heard of you. I guess you're not that famous."

"Not compared to really famous people," I say. "Like, not compared to Angelina Jolie."

"I'll say," he snorts. "But then who is? Anyways, this girl, I guess really a lady—I said to her, What's the use of being a poet. You don't make any money until you're dead, then your family gets it all. She says to me, 'I don't do it for money I do it for love, just like you do.' She'd come every day to buy stuff for her supper; I guess she really liked it here. She's gone now, her week's up, but before she went she gave me this. I was really impressed. I took it right down to my friend Jake, who frames things; he did me a favor, framed it right there while I waited. It's heavy, I'll hold it for you while you read."

I reach into my purse for my glasses and approach Rick and the framed text.

Such beautiful produce
Displayed with love and pride
Red tomatoes, yellow squash, green peppers
The minute I walked in, I knew I'd found
A special place.

The poem goes on for another twenty lines, praising Rick and his fruits and vegetables. All I can think of to say is "she's got really nice handwriting," but I know that's not what he wants to hear. Rick is beaming. In the time it's taken me to read the poem, he's grown younger by twenty years. Forty perhaps. He's a boy, but not his mother's son.

"That's really nice, Rick," I say. "You should be really proud."

"I guess she really appreciated, well, not me, but you know, what I do. What I stand for. I wanted to say to some of my ex-girlfriends, see, not everybody thinks I'm such a complete asshole."

"Of course, I've never met the poet laureate," Rick's mother says. "As far as I'm concerned she might be a mirage."

"Does a mirage write poetry?" Rick says, returning to his chronological age, but with an adolescent's petulance as an overhang. "Does a mirage make something you can frame?"

"All I'm saying is I never laid eyes on the lady," Lorraine says.

"There's a lot you never laid eyes on, mom. More than I could even begin to tell you."

I feel the need for an intervention. "Well, I think it's lovely," I say. "Very thoughtful."

"And she's a professional," he says.

Rick carries my bags to the car. I open the hatchback. "I'm always on my guard with these hatchback things" he says. "I carried a lady's bags for her this one time, she was an old lady mind you, but I'm putting them in the car and she's not paying attention, she presses the button on her key and the thing comes right down on my head. I was lucky I didn't get a concussion. I'm a sadder but wiser man now, believe me."

"I'll be careful," I say, "I would never want anything like that to happen."

"Oh, I know," he says. "Where are you off to now?"

"I'm going to swim in the lake."

"Larkspur Lake?"

"Yes, I like it a lot."

"I tried it once. Came down with a terrible case of swimmer's ear. You go there every day?"

"Mostly."

"Maybe you've seen the daughter of one of my exes. She takes her kids there every day. Megan. Long brown hair, slightly overweight, well, let's be honest, more than slightly, two little boys, around five or six."

"I'm not sure," I say.

But Rick won't give it up. "You must have seen her. Long brown hair, a tattoo with some kind of Chinese writing on her leg, drives a red pickup. I've done a lot of stupid things in my life, but I know I was a good thing for Megan. She says to me, 'Rick, if I ever have a good relationship with a guy, it's because of the way I saw you were so nice to my mother.' The guy she's with is a real good guy. She's had some hard times, and he's not working right now, this economy is murder on everyone. But they're trying, I think they'll make it."

I can tell that it's important to Rick that I've seen her. So I lie. It's a fault of mine. If someone seems to want something very much, I feel I have to give it to him.

If Rick wants me to have seen Megan that much, I'll pretend I have. I remember my last encounter with someone fitting Megan's description. I was getting out of the water when I heard a woman's voice shouting, "You lay a hand on my fucking kid again, I'll fucking kill you." These words were spoken by an overweight woman with long brown hair, the mother of two boys, around five or six. She had some sort of tattoo: I don't know if it was Chinese writing. I don't know what she drove.

But then I often saw another overweight woman with long brown hair and a tattoo; she also had two little boys, and she was tender with both of them, encouraging the little one to put his face in the water, praising the older one's dog paddle, his frog kick.

I can see Rick wants me to provide details. It is up to me which details I provide. This is, after all, my job. It's what I do. It's up to me which of the two women I choose to be Megan.

"They're a nice family," I say. "She's really good with the kids. The older one really looks out for the little one."

"That's good," Rick says. "I'm really glad for her. It's one of the things in the world that makes me feel good."

Happy with a job well done, a job I did as well as or better than the poet, I take my place behind the wheel.

"Don't work too hard," he says, "Remember, with what you do for a living, you won't be rich till you're dead."

ROBERT FARNSWORTH
Archive

Codices, caxtons, concordances—
your books, dusted, rearranged,
reshelved. But it's what falls
out of them most fascinates:
feathers, letters, fortunes,
tickets, baseball, post- and birthday cards stashed among the savored
or as-yet-unfinished pages. What
would get you back to *that* one?
A prison term perhaps, or the long
convalescence you have sometimes
thought you craved. The hands
that left these scraps behind, though,
aren't yours anymore. So you'd
have to start again. The half-read or
meant-to-be-read ones keep their
air of offering, while others
instantly flash their best ideas
or scenes across the mind. They
were so you. Or vice versa.
And into all these various books
someone (who was once you)
stuffed the quotidian confetti
of times when a volume went
with you in a bag. Finding these
is imagining a prior life,
a boy's life, which didn't quite
imagine this one. Fossil life,
shadow life, descanted over someone's
lasting words. Then, slipped down
toward the binding of some Dinesen,

a dozen lines of your own. Lines,
not notes. Whether prompted or just
tucked there, certainly "writing."
So earnest, so intended beside
the weird souvenirs, those sketchy
on-the-wing suggestions, lively
and transient as sparrows. Nothing
even to pity in those lines, seen
clearly at last in the company
of leavings. Which, of course,
you leave (this time deliberately)
behind, interleaved with those pages
you'd read and kept and meant to read,
like fingers locked in prayer; of old
allegiances the lost bright flags.
You leave them all, everything but
your own lines, which, with hilarious
relief, you tear up, very small.

ROBERT FARNSWORTH

Theatre

After the second act blacks out, you head to the lobby,
to feel the crowd stream around you, bearing secret
energies, as through water heaves a sullen wave, as
through the flag speaks a jubilance of wind. When you

stop near a table of brochures, a fat, sunburned boy
looks (instantly sizing you) up and says, "Can't get away
from people like us, huh?" Who sent *him?* From so far
around probability's bend he's almost part of the play.

Stunned then in the ghostly hush as lights go down
and actors take their places, as the scissoring whispers
die away, you feel, in a little upsurge of wonder,
that though you always make it look so in crowds, you

don't really want to get away from anyone, no; they
are the guarantors, corroborators, fellow believers,
among nature's strewn or the stage's contrived shadows.
They have to be there, those you keep your secrets from—

some days for their own good, some days for yours.
For all your cherished solitude, it is their presence makes
meaning of the chisel of October air thrust beneath
a grimy window, that poignantly invests a stagehand's

dark, anonymous stride across the boards to move furniture.
When the set blazes again, it will almost seem that you
know these actors, that they know you, elementally as kin.
But you keep thinking about those people who strike & reset

the scene, who'll keep their own good company after
the houselights come back up, and whom you'll never
get to tell of that Nova Scotian great aunt you are
remembering (O why now?) in the dark, who married

so young to clear the house for her brother's bride,
and who fondly recalled from decades back the village
washing days in June, when huge, slow banners of quilt
would wave and ripple, rinsing in a cold river's current.

STEPHEN GIBSON
Life Study

Viareggio bus station, Italy

He lifts him like they're wrestlers in the ring
or like in Pollaiuolo's *Hercules*
and Antaeus, only neither of these
guys is a hero and both have been drinking
all morning—this isn't the Uffizi
and what they're doing isn't in a painting:
it's a park, James Taylor's going to sing
tonight in Lucca, people around me
are also waiting for their bus to swing
around that corner where, under the trees,
their drivers are on a break—but these
guys inhabit a sphere that has nothing
to do with music: the one whose back may bend in
half shoves a forearm into the mouth of a lion.

DOREEN GILDROY
Celestial Room

I remember when I was four
a book seemed from heaven
and then, when I was eight,
it seemed a field.

*

How large the world has become,
the thoughts, capable.
I wanted to look at that, just that.

*

I thought I would never speak again.

But there are books, transformed,
and souls
that take time to recognize
the speaking, and which voice.

BOB HICOK

a bouquet of violence

black-eyed susans
sound abused, as if the night
beats flowers up and needs help
loving as people love
who sign letters
xoxoxoxo, which reminds me
of football coaches
showing massive men
how to destroy
massiver men on a chalkboard
at halftime. if you
are a flute thrown out a window
on the way to montgomery,
before the misery
of landing, there's a second
when you play your own tune.
then a kid comes along
on a bike and holds
your bends and scrapes,
your shiny bits, looks up
the road and down the road, sensing
she is at the far end
of a rope coming to pull her
out. so when her mother's
boyfriend squeaks her door
open, she is ready
to think of the knife
under her pillow
as a friend, the only breeze
on a hot day. beats me,
we say.
blackandblue, blackandblue.

BOB HICOK

Aubade shaped like breasts or arrows

Mistgreen maple leaves just twenty feet
from my looking, my remembering
         an equally soft morning
         in Monterosso, woman with left hand
            in sea, right hand
            cupping a baby's head
                to breast, how feminine
                it seems, the support, this mist
            rounding sharpness
            from bird chatter, this wombing
of fence, of farm, of distance
inviting me to wonder
         how they do it, the women
         who explode themselves
            to tempest a mosque,
            a soldier, a day
                in Baghdad and Netanya,
                scattering bits of hip,
            of skull for kids
            to find while I
        gather feathers and sticks
        to make a doll
for my niece of feathers
and quiet and sticks

BOB HICOK
Tree of life

There's something casual
about maple leaves. They're almost mittens,
in the first place. They refuse to stand
for the national anthem. And when it rains,
as it rained last night, a rain I listened to
on the floor, a rain as delicate
as a shoplifter, they're moved
by each raindrop and resist
each raindrop, creating a sound
that's both adamant and pliant,
a whispered "here I am"
to the petting sky. In the country,

I can stand naked in the rain
and still run for the senate one day.
Who would know: some slugs.
Not even the wires that bring us coal light
are watching. But I'm not suited
to making law or breathing money,
I'd find it hard to give corporations
what they want. I'd say no
a lot and get tired of saying no
a lot, and drink, and do drugs, senator drugs,
which are probably very good, very
democratic. One night, I'd stumble

into the rain and strip my no-suit off,
I'd wonder how my maple
is doing back home, if she misses me, if trees
have gender, if gender
engenders an imperative tension

in the procreative drive, and walk naked
past all the Smithsonians, all those buildings
with art and dinosaurs, not understanding life
any better than when I was seven
and thought the moon meant everything
it said. The moon, you know, goes through the motions
too. For all my narcissism, I find it hard
to remember I'm alive. But right now,
I remember I end on the tips of everything I see
or begin. Rain. I see rain. I see sun
wearing a disguise of water
to tell the truth.

AMY HEMPEL
Greed

Mrs. Greed had been married for forty years, her husband the cuckold of all time. A homely man with a notable fortune, he escorted her on errands in the neighborhood. It was a point of honor with Mrs. Greed to say she would never leave him. No matter if her affection for him was surpassed by her devotion to others. Including, for example, my husband. If she was home at night in her husband's bed, did he care what she did with her days?

I was the one who cared.

Protected by men, money, and a lack of shame, Mrs. Greed had long been able to avoid what she had coming. She had the kind of glee that meant men did not think she slept around, they thought she had joie de vivre; they thought her a libertine, not a whore.

She had the means to indulge impetuous behavior and sleep through the mornings after nights she kept secret from her friends. She traveled the world, and turned into the person she could be in other places with people she would never see again.

She was many years older than my husband, running on the fumes of her beauty. Hers had been a conventional beauty, and I was embarrassed by my husband's homage to it. Running through their rendezvous: a stream of regret that they had not met sooner.

He asked if she had maternal feelings for him. She said she was not sure what he wanted to hear. She told him she felt an erotic mix of passion and tenderness. If he wanted to think the tenderness maternal, let him.

When they met, he said, he had not hidden the fact that she looked like his mother, a glamorous woman who had been cruel to him and died when he was a boy. He had not said this to underscore her age, nor did she think it a fixation. She would have heard it as she felt it was intended: as a compliment, an added opportunity to bind them together. She would have been happy to be the good mother, as well as the ultimate sensate. And see how her pleasure-seeking brought pleasure to those around her!

A thing between them: green apples. Never red, always green. I knew when my husband had entertained Mrs. Greed because a trio of baskets in the kitchen would be filled with polished green apples. My husband claimed to like the look of them; I never saw him eat one. As soon as they started to soften and turn brown, I would throw them out. And there would be the basket filled so soon again.

He told me he got them from the Italian market in town. But I checked, and the Italian market does not carry green apples. What the green apples meant to them, I don't know, don't want to know. But she brought them each time she entered our house, and I felt that if I had not thrown the rotting ones out, he would have held on to every one of them. The way he fetishized these apples—it made him less attractive to me.

Mrs. Greed convinced her young lover, my husband, that she was "not the type" to have "work" done, but she had had work done. She must have had a high threshold for pain. She could stay out of sight for the month or more of healing after each procedure. She had less success hiding the results of surgery on her spine. She claimed her athleticism had made it necessary, claimed a "sports injury" to lessen the horror of simple aging. But she could not hide the stiffness that followed, a lack of elasticity that marked her an old woman who crossed the street slowly in low-heeled shoes. I watched her cross the street like this, supported by my husband.

Maybe that was why she liked to hear complaints about his other women, that they were spoiled and petty, gossips who resented his involvement with her. Because he would not keep quiet about such a thing. At first, she felt the others had "won" because they could see him at any time. Then she saw that their availability guaranteed he would tire of them. They were impermanent, and she knew it before they did. So however much he pleaded with her to leave her husband, or at least see *him* more often, Mrs. Greed refused. It galled me that he wanted her more than she wanted him.

I listened to them often. I hooked up the camera to the computer when I was at home alone. For $200 I'd bought a hidden surveillance camera that was fitted into a book. I did not expect it to work. I left it next to the clock on the nightstand. I did not pay the additional $75 that would have showed them to me in color. But the ninety-degree field of view was adequate for our bedroom, and sound came in from up to 700 feet. Had this not worked so well, I would have stood in line for the camera that came hidden in a ceiling-mounted smoke detector.

Usually the things they said were exchanges of unforeseen delight, and riffs of gratitude. But the last time I listened to them, my husband said something clever. Mrs. Greed sounded oddly winsome, said she sometimes wished the two of them had "waited." My husband told her they could *still* wait—they could wait a day, a week, a month—"It just won't be the *first* time," he said.

How she laughed.

I said to myself, "I am a better person!" I am a speech therapist who works with children. Parents say I change their lives. But men don't care about a better person. You can't photograph virtue.

I found the collection of photographs he had tried to hide. I liked that the photos of herself she brought to him were photos from so long ago. Decades ago. She wears old-fashioned bathing suits aboard sailboats with islands in the faded background. Let her note that the photographs of me that my husband took himself were taken in this bed.

Together, they lacked fear, I thought, to the extent that she told him to bring me to dinner at her house. With her husband. Really, this was the most startling thing I heard on playback. Just before the invitation, she told him she would not go to bed with the two of us. My husband was the one to suggest it. As though the two of us had talked it over, as if this were something I wanted! I heard her say, "I have to be the queen bee." Saw her say it.

She would not go to bed with us, but she would play hostess at dinner in her home.

I looked inside my closets, as though I might actually go. What does one wear for such an occasion? The corset dress? Something off the shoulder? Something to make me look older? But no dress existed for me to wear to this dinner. The dress had to do too much. It had to say: I am the sexy wife, and I will outlast you. It had to say: You are no threat to my happiness, and I will outlive you.

Down the street from our house, a car waited for Mrs. Greed. I knew, because I had taken note before, that a driver brought her to see my husband when I visited clients out of town. Was there a bar in the back of this car? I couldn't tell—the windows had a tint. Maybe she would not normally drink, but because there was a decanter of Scotch and she was being driven some distance at dusk, maybe she poured herself a glass and toasted her good luck?

This last thought reassured me. How was it this felt normal to me, to think of her being driven home after a tumble with my husband? I guess it depends on what you are used to. I knew a man who found Army boot camp "touching," the attention he received from the drill sergeant, the way the Army fed him daily. It was a comfort to him to know what each day would bring.

I felt there could be no compensation for being apart from my husband. Not for me, and not for her.

I knew I was supposed to be angry with *him*, not with her. She was not the first. She was the first he would not give up. But I could not summon the feelings pointed in the right direction. I even thought that killing her might be the form my *self*-destruction took. Had to take that chance. I tried to go cold for a time—when I thought of him, when I thought of her. But there was a heat and richness to what I conceived that made me think of times I was late to visit a place that my friends had already seen. When you discover something long after others have known it, there is a heady contentment that comes.

What I heard on the tapes after that: their relaxed relentlessness, impersonal intimacy, the air of resuming a rolling conversation that *we* had not been having. As though living in another dimension, a dimension I thought I could live in too, once. Just take me there. Just teach me the new rules.

Watching them on camera I thought: What if I'm doing just what I'm supposed to be doing? And then I thought: I am.

The boys said they would give me a sign.

It was money well spent. With what I saved not needing to film in color, and knowing I would not need the standard two-year warranty, I had enough to pay the thuggish teens a client's son hung out with. The kid with the stutter had hinted he needed m-m-money. I will even give them a bonus—I will let them keep the surveillance camera hidden in the book after they send me the final tape.

Mrs. Greed does not live so far away that I will miss the ambulance siren.

And what to make of this? The apples my husband "bought," the green ones from the Italian market that does not carry green apples—I ate one on the front steps of our house and threw the core into pachysandra. The next morning the core I had thrown was on the top step where I had been sitting when I ate it. I threw it again, this time farther out so it lodged in pine needles alongside the road in front of our house. The morning after that, today, the core was back in place on the top step.

Boys.

I thought: Let's see what happens next.

We have so many apples left.

EDWARD HIRSCH

September Song

One moment you were tossing me a football
in the empty field behind your house
and the next I was getting clobbered
by a linebacker and run over by a safety.

Forty years vanished in that instant
when the pigskin touched my hands,
which are still soft, and the defensive end
straightened me out with a forearm shiver.

I never liked blocking down on tackles
from the strong side, or kneeling in mud,
but I loved taking out an unsuspecting corner.
My falls were seasons for cracking bones.

I remember standing in the shower after practice
and discovering the bruises breaking out
all over my body, like mushrooms
sprouting from the ground after a hard rain

and then creaking home on the feeder road
that curved between Eden's highway
slowly drowning with traffic
and a family farm slated for extinction.

I tried running patterns in my mind—
the flag, the fly, the quick pass over the middle—
but there was no darkness like the darkness
of night falling on Niles Center Road.

One moment you were tossing me a football—
my body remembers—and the next
I was catching a glimpse of the moon
slipping over a smokestack in the distance.

In the end, it was the moon that saved me,
a ghostly spiral, a rising crescent
that split a seam in the clouds
and promised to lead me out of there.

DAVID KIRBY
Baby Handle

Samurai sword-fighting lesson, Tokyo

We're using the *iaitō* or "practice sword" now
    as opposed to the *shinken* or "live sword" which
looks as though it can cut through lampposts
        and is "hungry for the flesh of its owner,"
says smiling Sakaguchi-san through a translator,
    which is why I'm getting lots of unintentional laughs

when I keep saying, "Can we just check the edges
    one more time before we start?" It's impossible
not to swagger when you're wearing a sword
        and are Western, though the Japanese don't swagger;
they just scurry up to one another and start hacking.
    Well, not "scurry": the idea, we learn, isn't to win,

it's to not lose, because when you're trying to win,
    you're rushing in heedlessly and making all kinds
of mistakes, whereas when you're trying to not lose,
        you're taking your time and waiting for your enemy
to screw up so you can exploit his error, presuming
    your opponent is considerate enough to be heedless

and mistake-prone. You want to attain *heijōshin*,
    in other words, which is one of those untranslatable
Japanese philosophical concepts best rendered here
        as "mindfulness" and which Sakaguchi-san wants me
to have when we are sparring with the *bokken*
    or "wooden sword" and I try to clobber him.

"Uh, uh!" he says, wagging his finger at me and then,
  using his only English of the day, "Baby
handle. Baby handle!" And he takes my forearm and caresses it
    and even puts my hand to his face and closes his eyes
as though he is putting a child to sleep. Goodnight, baby!
  Sleep tight, little Japanese baby that was once my arm

and is trying to be heedless and error-prone instead
    of mindful as we change positions and Sakaguchi-san
draws his *bokken* from his *obi* and advances on me,
      and I remember how the most famous
samurai of them all, Miyamoto Musashi, once asked his disciple
    Jotarō what his goal was, and when Jotaro said,

"To be like you!" Musashi-san replied, "Uh, uh!
  Your goal is too small! You should aspire to be like
Mount Fuji, with such a broad and solid foundation
          that nothing can move you, not even the strongest
earthquake! You will then see all things clearly:
    not just things happening near you but forces that shape

all events," and as Sakaguchi-san seizes the wooden sword
    with two hands and raises it above his head, I think
of Shakespearean actor Mark Rylance, of whom
        it's been said that he seems to have more time
than anyone else, like an athlete—like Michael
      Jordan, say, because if it takes you three seconds to shoot

a lay-up, it seems as though Jordan-san is in the air for ten
    seconds, fifteen, more. The *bokken*
in my teacher's double-handed grip has reached the end of its arc,
          and now that he's bringing it down,
I remember as well that John Berryman essay on Shakespeare
      with its recollection of *Twelfth Night,* in which Laurence

Olivier as Sir Toby Belch and Alec Guinness
        as Sir Andrew Aguecheek played the drinking scenes
so slowly that, in Berryman's words, "they might almost
                have been dead," as though Hamlet himself had told
them to "speak the speech…trippingly on the tongue;
        but if you mouth it, as many of your players do, I had

as lief the town-crier spoke my lines. Nor do not
        saw the air too much with your hand thus, but use all gently;
for in the very torrent, tempest, and, as I may say,
                whirlwind of your passion, you must acquire and beget
a temperance that may give it smoothness."
        Baby handle, good sirs! O for a Muse of fire

that would ascend the brightest heaven of invention!
        And were I a samurai, then at my heels, leashed in
like hounds, should famine, sword, and fire crouch
                for employment! Bang! Sakaguchi-san raps me
smartly with his *bokken*, and I realize that
        if he had been using his *shinken* or even his *iaitō*,

then my head would now be in two neat pieces.
        Banished to the sideline, I watch as he spars with another
student and see how, when the sword is falling
                on Sakaguchi-san's own head, he looks at it for what
seems like minutes, weighing his options
        until he picks the right one and then flicking

his opponent's weapon to one side as a king on a battlefield
        might unhorse another or a baby put aside his toy and take up
the crown his mother has brought him
                as she brushes back his hair and kisses him and says,
Take this, wear it, and gestures toward the wide world
        behind her and says, Take this too, it's yours.

MARK KRAUSHAAR
Arthur

Anger doesn't catch the light like laughter,
but with my friend it seems to crowd him,
seems to complicate his neck and jaw.
It's not just that.
It's made him fat.
We've only walked two blocks
and he's wheezing when we reach Walgreens.
A wind-fixed scent of diesel passes.
I hate my job, he says, I'm tired,
and my friends don't call.

Of course, there's always the traffic and the weather
and the war but it used to be the slob next door
and before they split up it was always
the missus: no zip, no spark,
no spunk, too calm by half—
calm when his car died, calmer when
the lawn caught fire,
still calmer in the primal act.
But it's not the job he can't stand
(though it is and he can't) it's the people
and the pay and we pause and later back home
finally closing my eyes there's the usual slow motion
stars and ambient blues and unblacks and I think
of this friend, so sad, and peevish and pudgy,
collapsing slowly into himself,
an arithmetic of battered will
and bungled choice.
And who's exempt?
Hopeful or angry or afraid, it's
being here, living here, and going along

at the center of a perfect, unattainable present
as if some bruised and tumbling private sky were
moving in, the soft, random patter of rain.

MARK KRAUSHAAR
The Cat and the Fiddle

In the scene where the cow jumps
over the moon the little dog laughs
with his mouth wide open.
Comforted by the same thirty words
he's heard fifty times the boy leans sideways
into his mother.
Before this they'd walked by the water.
Before that they'd spread their blanket on
the grassy bank, and before that
the mother looked straight ahead and thought
of how she might change her whole life starting,
starting soon—
and how like an adult.
And how like these two to fish and say poems
at the wrong time completely.
Before the short drive to the lake,
before certain words at the stove,
they'd sat with the dad in the kitchen.
And couldn't the boy just listen, for once?
No. No, he wouldn't know good luck or good news
if they'd spanked him in unison.
You see here is a child who any more to keep
after what good would it do?
Meat loaf night.
The lights of the cabana shine over the water.
The mother and son sip warm Cokes on the pier.
Now the boy leans sideways resting his head.
And how like the fat cat to fiddle
and play like nothing's amiss,
and how like the grinning dish to lift high
its inconsequent legs and speed away
when its place is at home.

Her Dream

We were arguing about children.
I was pleading,
        "Something could be done, stars could be fixed
        above their hands—"

And then a star-shaped pattern of skin
in a surgical basin.

To be fixed
        to every child's face, ironed over it

        like a wrapper.

BRIDGET LOWE

Anti-Pastoral

Your green Arcadian hills do not interest me.
The bird-bright eyes of every bird cared for,
the way it is promised, the way it is written,
everyone fat on their share of sun and seed.

But I don't see you in the dark streak of a cat
crossing the street or the regal skunk in summer's heat
that strolls the sidewalk after dark, stopping to look at me
before moving on to its home under a neighbor's porch,
pushing its black-white weight through the lattice work.

I don't see you in a head of lettuce, decapitated and wet
at the grocery store, singing in Orphic dissonance.
I look out at your trees and see the night
I watched my mind rise up and leave
the body's bed, the skin of the moon in your teeth.

I begged you to make the mule of my mind
come back. Do you remember what you said?
Nothing. And in the silence after that—
my head without my body, singing on the riverbed.

BRIDGET LOWE

The Pilgrim Is Bridled and Bespectacled

World, I honor you.
After everything
we've been through

I honor you and take you with me
up the mountainside
where we will live
in wonderment.

I take you to the desert
where we shrivel like worms
and become tongues
for other people to kiss with.

World, there are two baskets
on my back.
Fill them. Fill them with fruit
and more fruit.

Or fill them with whatever
is customary
but tell me it is fruit.
Call it something good.

World, some have satisfied their thirst.
But I am the crying-out animal
who can see in the dark.
Forgive me.

BRIDGET LOWE

The Pilgrim Looks at the World from Above

I want this life, full of dogs and people.
The trick is not stopping.
The dead sleep like bugs tucked into matchboxes

while the living imitate life
within the confines of pink and green lines
denoting states.

And I see you wandering the labyrinth
of your dumb animal existence,
your body warm, seeking exit.

Somewhere a man takes out his teeth.
The body is a series of reductions, losses.

Parasitic longing worms its way into his back.
He rolls onto his other side
and turns off the light, seeking comfort.

Seeking comfort you have done everything
but die.

I see you turning corners and pulling at your hair.
I see you weeping against the wall
that is always there.

And in dreams I dare to see you
delivered into an open field, a vast space
on the map where a creek flows

and nothing can stop it, the feeling,
the love you have for your life,
for your very own animal body

which has delivered you there
in time, just in time.

Cremains

Her kitchen is filled with the neighbors' dishes—all well-meaning, pity-stained, uncleaned. She can't quite think, so she shuffles about the house, marveling at the strangeness. Touching the bill pile, a bruised spot in the oak banister, his fleece jacket on a coat rack, the cannon-shaped back of a wedding gift mixer, the crumbling scone on a plate that isn't hers. What thoughts she has come in images, snapping like those Buddhist prayer flags, frayed and scribbly: images of her sister-in-law hemming new pants seconds before they left for the funeral home, making everyone wait, then trying them on again with the higher heels. Ass-suctioned slacks, but they were black. Images of Sam spilling off the old red leather couch, drunk. He'd been drunk since she called him two hours after it happened, in that stretch of night when a ringing phone can only mean emergency. Maybe he was drunk then too. Images of people she vaguely knew, coming in waves, all murmuring sorrys and squinting at her. Perhaps she was too composed. Everyone wants the spectacle of grief instead of its reality, which is this—this floating in star-gas, bewildered by strangeness.

She sees herself beside him, sitting at the dinner table with the coupling ones, the newly loved, and asking how they met. Nate had one knee up, his hands clasped around it. They'd planned this meal weeks ago and forged ahead, pretending they were speaking to each other still. Marriage has these odd terrains. Act as if. Act as if you can stand each other. The new couple told their story as a fluid duet: she smiled at him and said she was trying to catch a cab. His eyes brushed her lips as he described struggling with his bass and the snow that gets hip-deep on city curbs. The story's still new to them, they're still writing it; they were giving off sparks as they twined sentences. Mira's smile was too tight, but she wore it anyway. She leaned to refill their wine glasses, then got up to check the apple crostata in the oven. The couple's story wasn't long enough to occupy the tired evening. So of course they asked, "How did you two meet?"

That moment scratched. It wasn't possible to look at each other yet. They'd been in the queerness for days. When she looked, she could see his raspy hair, his gone-gooey chin, the cracks from too much sun, the blankness of him. God knows what he saw. She's decomposing too. But that's not the point. They were seeing too familiarly. They weren't seeing at all. It was that marital fugue, the unendurable one.

Tell your story. Give the urtext of your love. Instead of this simulacra.

The new couple pulsed light, expectantly. She was tucked under her lover's ambling arm.

"Oh, it's so long and not very interesting." Mira emptied the wine bottle into their glasses, turned toward the coffee machine.

Nate flicked lint from his knee. He was the story's teller. Over time, it becomes a story only one person tells. Mira admired how he made subtle changes each time, not to alter the truth, but to keep it from being mere recitation, adding tiny improvisations or a nearly lost detail that brought it all back to life. She loved hearing him tell it.

Silence. Mira asked the couple about a mutual friend as she tamped the espresso deftly, hiding a bubble of panic.

She can't remember. She can't remember their story. It's like letting someone else drive. You forget the way.

Now she wanders about the house feeling Nate's presence, like warm spots in water. When she reaches the dining room, something flickers tonguely and she realizes she's left a candle burning overnight and all day, into this murky dusk. Christ. That was dangerous. She wets her thumb and forefinger, extinguishes it. Enjoys the smoke and the slight buzz in her fingertips. Images of the man who sat at the end of the couch, saying nothing. The woman in a slit-sleeve dress sat next to him, nearly thigh-to-thigh, but she spoke with someone else while taking bites of chocolate-dipped strawberries. A few sat knee-splayed on the floor, also near. People seemed to need to touch. But the man on the end of the couch spoke with no one and sat for hours and said not one thing. How lovely to be a man, Mira thought for an instant, admiring his silence, his solitude in this mob. Images of people hugged in clumps on the stairs, coats piled on the banister, the folding wooden chairs no one used because they seemed so borrowed. Images of mountains of food. Deviled eggs, those stuffed mushrooms, something with cucumbers and dill on tiny squares of rye bread, a platter of cut fruit and one of slithery meat folded into ripples. How odd to have food. How odd to be in your own home, unable to move because there are people everywhere, drinking and eating. Images of her mother-in-law briskly cleaning, arranging apple slices on a plate artfully, and of her sister-in-law touching her collarbones as she laughed.

Mira never called them in-laws before the wake. It sounds so begrudging, she used to say. But everything had shifted. His mother kept saying it must be God's will and wearing the same smile she did every Thanksgiving: a lush but distracted smile. Images of that. And of his father's wake, much like this one with too much food and the house oddly spotless and the mourners shocked. A medical error, his mother had said then. Mira accepted the way his mother hugged her by the hip, nodded somberly, buck-it-uply, like a fellow soldier widow. Mira knows now: flawed hearts. The world is flooded with them. She can't think, so won't. Whether these are deceits, whether she would have lived differently had they known, whether Nate did know—she can't think about any of this.

Grief expands and contracts like breath, distancing everything. She bobs among the stars, a lost balloon, something a startled child let loose. The phone rings constantly. She's so tired of everyone singing into the machine, *Just checking in*, all the awkward sympathy, the forced jokes. Images of too much hilarity at the wake and not enough now. Images of the man on the end of the couch growing a slow scowl just before he crumpled into sobs, and still no one comforted him. That's what self-sufficiency gets you. Mira was across the room at the time, standing next to a woman with a rubbery face, a onetime colleague of Nate's, who was describing in intestinal detail her parents' deaths.

"The first home nurse was a total head case. Oh yes," she waved her hands gaily while Mira looked at the woman's wide mouth, globbed with orange, then looked at the man crying alone at the end of the couch, "she even left a filled diaper on the kitchen counter. I kid not! I would have fired her sooner, but she was too drunk to drive." Laughter with bits of food splatter, standing too close, telling too much. Images from the wedding day of her mother's best friend, both of them gin-soaked. The friend's lipstick was always botched—a wobbly smear around her mouth. *Drunko the Clown*, Nate dubbed her. It was one of their threads, part of the connective life tissue that held them together. If, while lying in bed not touching, Mira thought, Drunko the Clown, she would smile and turn toward him.

Images of an ancient woman in her wheelchair by the door at the funeral home. People occasionally leaning over the woman to shout, *Would you like something to drink?* Mira did not know who the old woman was, but went to sit on an ottoman near her. Held out one hand. The woman gripped it fiercely and never let go.

"You know, my first reaction when my son Geoff came to tell me the news," she shifted, peering at Mira, "he was so upset, he came over to my house, late at night, right into my bedroom and woke me. When he told me about Nate," the tiny woman paused for a breath, "my first reaction was *rage*."

Jesus, thought Mira, how perfect. An ancient woman feeling rage at a young man's death. They squeezed hands. The old woman then talked about her dogs at length, dogs with names like Spider and Bathsheba. This was how she knew Nate. Their families lived a few blocks apart. Her dog used to jump the fences and dodge cars to reach Nate's sunny pup, Stella. "It was a *true* love," the old woman said. "After Stella, they got another dog—I forget her name, but Nate called her Pomster, nasty dog—anyway, Spider wouldn't visit anymore. He never went back to their yard again."

Mira did not want to leave the woman, but someone came and gripped her shoulders, whispering, "There's someone here you need to—" Someone political, probably. Someone who could stand there next to Nate's body and still believe in power.

One night, she feels well enough to read Yeats for comfort, so she tries. She reads a line, then comes to minutes later and tries again. Too fractured yet. She blames the people. All the people who came and clogged her home and brain. People who came in two types: the ones who cried too much and the ones who laughed too much. And as she moved about the house, people touched her too much. With those looks. A pained love in those looks, but also disapproval. Why? Because she decided not to bury but to burn him? Because she's not a train wreck? Because he went instead?

Or maybe they can see what she is thinking.

Why does she feel lust, she wonders. Is that appropriate? For days, she thinks only of a man she used to fuck. She wants to call him. He's on his second wife now, or third, which is why they only fucked. Mira knew. Men come in two types: the ones who can't be faithful and the ones who can. The ones who can't tend to fuck like magicians. Mira grins, realizing this. The ones who can't are unselfish in bed and selfish everywhere else. Balances.

There are these porous moments in grief when it seems certain that the dead can hear the thoughts of the living. Mira's ashamed that Nate knows what she's thinking, ashamed that Nate knows before she does when she's drifted off into imagining her old lover hearing the news and calling—he has a gift for expressing concern—to insist on seeing her, on doing something to help. Or maybe he'll read it in the paper and just come to the house, though she wouldn't be able to do it in the house, not yet, so they'd have to go somewhere else. Which has appeal. She knows a cubicle in the library where they could meet, though it's impossible for her to be quiet with him. He cultivates her wildness. A bathroom sink is just high enough, he's got those long legs, so maybe a restaurant. She knows how game he'd be. Nate hasn't even been fed to the furnace yet and Mira is trilling with images, different bathrooms, different positions, this other man's hands.

But she knows it's like slipping on ice. The instinct is to reach out and grab; the assumption is that anything is more stable. She tries to think her way out of it, then slinks back to images. This man was an explicit kisser, an insister. He could hold her in midair as they hip-locked. Fuck it. She lets the images come. People often want the muck of mortalness right after a death. This, too, is instinct. And he's so attentive, it makes her feel swimmy. Sometimes she hated it, being visible to him. Nate's gaze was so different, with his mother's distraction in it. Or maybe it was just marriage. Scrims descend. Bathroom doors get left open. And sex becomes as curiously tender as his last breath.

Images of that. Of how hard he fell. As if he'd suddenly turned into a bag of earth. Though he convulsed in spasming waves afterward, the doctors later assured her he was already gone. It was just organs protesting the fact that the heart had halted. She had tried to push on his chest, to give him her breath. But his whole body was bucking. There was blood on her tongue from biting it, from trying to hold him still, from shouting: *This is not happening.*

Oh yes, she assures each anxious face asking, it was peaceful.

This is such a fucking lie. The spasms were violent. The organs were pissed. The body protests being suddenly done with. What about the years of running and motorcycles, music making and yoga, the years of organic farm produce and all the women in homemade skirts, women in red hair, women in drunken tears? What about all the guitars that body had bent over and the meals made to share with friends and the laundry done and the scars collected? One scar from the time he leaned plywood against a garage roof and climbed up with his skateboard. One from the kitchen knife, too blunt against the onion. One from the damned Pomeranian his mother hand-fed steak. One from an oven burn just after a big fight. She can't remember what the fight was about, but the burn left a raised welt across his wrist, like he'd slashed it. Scars from skiing and rock climbing and bike accidents, then shoulder surgeries. Scars from Denali and the two years it took to prepare for it. This body climbed Denali, which eats more souls than Everest. Denali, where a climber can flash freeze in seconds. She'd resented it: all the focus, the training, the expense of crevasse rescue classes and trips to climb Rainier, trips to practice climbing glaciated mountains and frozen waterfalls. Images of that. Of climbing a frozen waterfall. Of the truck jammed with gear as he left the driveway.

"Why?" she'd asked over pushed-away plates the night before his trip. If he didn't come back, she would need the answer.

"To merge with majestic immensity," he said.

Images of his hands on the stem of his glass as he said it, looking at her as though already immersed in Denali's wild beauty. What a solitary joy, she thought. So solitary it dissolves you. That must be what it's like to write a symphony or cross the desert. Or to be married. He was gone for six weeks and came back, banged and radiant, aged like Moses. Uncountable scars from that trip alone. How can you just discard a body like that, with so many stories in it?

In moments, it feels like the house is swallowing her. Sometimes she wishes she had a dog or a cat, any other presence. Instead there's only her strobing mind and periodic grief seizures, her animal sobs. Howling for what. The flowers keep arriving then dying, mail is mounding up by the phone, ignored, and decisions must be made, but she can't think. She wants to be with Nate when they feed him to the fires. She insists. They keep delaying it. The director has lost his solicitous cupped-hands posture and has started to be gross. Tells her about the smell, the noise, the brutality of organs and bones and flesh being burned, and how witnesses have vomited so hard they dehydrated. His pornographic morbidity fascinates. It's one of the few times she feels focused, actually. She stares at him while he flaps a freed hand and speaks without his mask. Evidently they're backed up with corpses. She must wait and he must hurry. Finally the time is set and the day opens its jaws and she gets up and showers and sits with coffee. Then the director leads her through the corridors without talking. She feels serene. Nate's body deserves a sentinel. His body is beloved.

The corridors are cold, the tile shoddy. They walk to an outbuilding through an underground tunnel. The incinerator looks industrial. The floors are stained cement. There is none of the caramel-brown couch and gas fireplace comfort of the funeral parlor. She will have to stand right here, the director signals insistently. She ignores him, drawing close enough to feel it, to feel the fact that the temperature toggles between 1,650 and 1,620 degrees. Now the man is telling her that the metal in the box's hinges and Nate's left shoulder won't burn, nor will any dental gold or his wedding ring or large bone fragments. The fragments will be separated to process again, for uniformity. After a cooling period, he explains, they sweep and rake and sweep again, to be sure they have all the cremains. He says cremains. What kind of word is that? Mira wonders if they bother to sweep so carefully when no one is witnessing. The director stands near until she tells him to leave.

She understands the need for solitary joy. After hearing Nate's answer, she didn't need to see the pictures he took on Denali to understand it.

There is not as much odor as she expected. The smells are oily, like a factory, not a body. The control panel has a dial that reads Throat Air Off, with an insistent red light beneath it. There is a concert of popping sounds, the sounds of bones cracking. It takes nearly four hours. They have to reposition him twice. She stares into the open flames when the oven is cracked so a man in heavy gloves can rake the glowing bones. There is something that looks like a hip or a skull. There is licking fire. There is all of this. It is so much more real than anything they fought about, anything she brooded over or doubted or declared intolerable. What could be more intolerable than this?

And yet every moment has these two sides, like the moon, the side you can see and the side that's in darkness. It was part of the moment they met in the street, after his dog almost got hit by a careening car. She wouldn't tell him her name. It was not a love story. They never are. It was a fleeing-from-love story that Nate remade, through grace and patience, a gift for love's solitariness—her spirit twinned, though she never understood that until this furnaced moment. Images of him laughing while she tried to ski. Images of him cradling Sam's newborn with awe. Images of the daft Rabbi at their wedding and his mother's rare tears. Images of him leaning forward to cut the crostata and tell their story, to tell it so movingly, with such an imbedded hymn of struggle and surrender, of effort—the things no one tells because they suggest love's failures instead of its summits—that it resolved her. That night they had orchestral sex. Five weeks later, he was cremains.

They are moments. Strung together. Like flags whose prayers are dispersed only when the script fades, the ends fray, the erasure takes place, feeding the wind its peace like seeds.

JYNNE DILLING MARTIN

Always Throw the First Fish Back Into the Sea

The world resembles a phantom vessel destined
to sail but never reach a port. The kidnapping victim

bound to a sawmill tries to loosen the ropes in vain
as electric sparks shower down, unsure if help is on the way.

Later in life he will apprentice with a sailor and learn
to pull apart every knot. I am not afraid of shackles

but dread the traps that precede them: the decoy duck,
the pitfall, the plainclothes officer posing as a friend.

Once imprisoned you can relax into your chains,
befriend the rats who will elect you as mayor,

you will have time to entertain their many complaints,
to feel the stones beneath you separately, round or pointed,

to chalk mark each day, but the difficult trick is to die
without thinking of betrayal, the quicksand under the bed.

If you can learn to not see all nets as snares, you can stroll
freely about the ship deck and say, this is the silver mist

hemming us in, there is the anchor ready to drop,
these are the rats who will flee if they sense we are sinking.

JYNNE DILLING MARTIN

The Fads and Fashions of Our Life and Times

The dancer's dying words: get my swan costume ready.
No one stirs from her bed. Elsewhere a hollowed pharaoh

lies with fingers and toes capped in golden thimbles
as a sandstorm thickens outside. A human-headed bird

evacuates his body by day and at night returns to nest
in his emptied stomach. The purpose of mummification

is to make a good first impression: even kings are anxious
when entering a crowded room. The dancer recalls

how blood drained from her pale lifted arms in the darkness
while she waited for the next curtain to rise, how vital

it seemed to smile. In the din of the afterparty it's hard
to hear: does she dislike the hyacinth or the asylum?

Harder and harder to say what will win over the rest;
like the barbarians who did not know how to feint

or retreat, some plow headlong into foreign fields
setting everyone behind them on fire. Others prepare

carefully for the new year with ointments and prayer,
thinking that will stave off demonic occupation. But

someday an invading army will seize each of our homes.
They will not understand our language, no, nor us them.

MICHAEL MILBURN
Divorcée

She accepts all invitations,
asking me what else she's
supposed to do. It's all you
can do, I tell her, apart from

staying home every night,
which is where I was when
she phoned from the party,
the kind I used to frequent

as part of my own new life,
but no longer do. I heard
the tinkling of drinks, music,
and laughter—the materials

for a life or the ruins of one,
depending how you look at it,
and her, building or burying,
depending how you look at it.

JAMES THOMAS MILLER
Who Can't Handle Me Is You

for Little Milton & Charlie Rich

Memphis, City of the Dead, City of Sun and blight,
Soulsville, rest stop for *hell they gone and run off.*
Tonight I dog you like a broken trombone. Twice
I've ended here on Union past midnight, brain looted
by morphine, the tremolo pinch of train steel across
the Frisco Bridge barbing my ear like a fever.
Twice here with the same girl for the same reason,
a formal on a steamboat, though the only thing formal
about us was our lust, the kind of phantom romance
reserved for teens, pulp novels, what's left before the prosthetic.
On the *Delta Queen*, surrounded by pretend friends,
mint juleps, we stood at the stern, watching numb
Arkansas stars glass the tide off Mud Island white.
These were my early twenties, a time I neither regret
nor admire. I courted spleen like a silent partner,
considered myself above the debutantes and their dates
dancing across the deck's antebellum-red carpet.
I wasn't. Both times, after the parties ended,
she and I found our way past the Lorraine, past Rayford's,
to Ernestine and Hazel's, where as if by script some
half-tight frat boy or all-thumbs drunk eventually
played "Break Up" on the jukebox and for 151 seconds,
I thought fate was more than loose reins slapping
the neck of a pale, runaway horse. It was voices,
the pitched A when she said my name, the strained
reverb in the hollows of Charlie Rich's acetate lament,
contrails strung like a diddley bow over the river,
back and forth, from Ardent to Stax, Poplar to Central,
traffic stalled in the key of C, the hoofed backbeat of
carriages at the Peabody, all converged into a single drone,

each sound grown loud together, then stopping, with one
click of the needle, the entire room, her and me silent.
We walked back to the hotel, the Mississippi a chicken snake
hissing us along cobblestone, and made love, our bodies
urged forward by habit, the weight of where they'd been.

Looking at an Old Photograph

A well-made thought, a coin.
It must have been the vista we were after
since nobody's in it. But where was it?
It was a clear day, though, look.
We must have loved the way it opened out,
suggesting some idea, maybe lunch,
we thought it led to, without which
our life might have been (horrible thought) over.
It wasn't, of course, but I wish I knew
where it was I must have said to you,
"You've got to take a picture of this."
We must have rushed back to the hotel, glad,
and then back where we came from, changed
in ways too closely seen to be recalled.

ROGER MITCHELL

Mouth

Maybe nothing is meant to be seen so,
but when I saw your mouth, your mouth alone,
neither in sleep nor silenced by thought, fear,
astonishment at our selves, for we were
alone, at last, in bed, not far from sleep,
I thought I saw the consequence of things,
the having to prevail over the hours,
in your lips, thinned by a nameless straining
after bliss, lips, as the poet says, I've kissed,
and not known then whether to abandon
what's gone already or seek in the small
sag at the corner of your mouth where you
park your sadness, or your incipient mustache,
treasures, as I have, I will always find.

Overnight at Key West

Crack in the silence,
blades of green
a warbler leaps through.

The same room,
roses on the wallpaper,
a deep old tub.

And I've opened the blinds.
Stripes of light
corrugate the bedclothes.

HONOR MOORE
Sunblind at Huayapam

Through blue glass, a table painted blue, roses vermilion,
Amber tumblers, candlesticks, a mirror darkening until all

Grays in oncoming light. Goats bleat, radioblare, a gunshot.
Past the celosia, a tree where yellow birds feed; heat and wind

From the mountains. Close your eyes and retinas scald
The window crimson, mullions bright of orangeskin

Lit from within. Siren, airplane, air enlivened by dogs barking,
Then a tremor from the interior as if the tree meant to fall

Or this dark could ever be complete. In the cathedral, saints
Arc downward through gilded vaulting, mouths agape, supplicate

Arms outstretched as if to thwart a tumble into mortality, then
We are outside, the actual sky blue, nothing to foreclose any act

Of reaching. Or it's night, the only sound breath, until the dogs start,
Each overcoming another, as if the message might get through.

A Memo From Your Temp

I am sitting behind a desk, not my desk, maybe your desk, watching the clock. That woman who works in the next cubicle has her radio tuned to NPR. "All Things Considered" has come on. This is good, this means that we are getting toward the end of things. The work day, I mean. On the radio Susan Stamberg is talking to a farmer and his wife in Nebraska who are watching their possessions being auctioned off. Susan's sympathetic. So am I. More so than Susan (and, I'm guessing, you), because Susan's probably never watched what was hers turn into somebody else's, whereas I have.

I get up to get a drink of water. I don't have to worry about making conversation with people at the water cooler because now people bring their own water, in bottles. Bottles they've paid cash money for, and suck on all day, like big babies. This is something I can't get used to. Well, there's a lot I'm not used to. I've been out of the "workplace" for a long time. I am here now as a temp. I am here everywhere in my life as a temp.

When I come back into your little "private" space, I see your daughter's second-grade school picture in that cheesy sea-shell frame your mother-in-law probably gave you last Christmas. I also see my new jacket hanging over the back of the chair. Seeing the jacket gives me a jolt. I bought it recently at a thrift store. It is brown suede and cost me fifteen dollars. I didn't realize why I'd wanted it until this minute. It is almost the exact same jacket that an old boyfriend of mine, a boy named Ray, gave me when I was about twenty-two. It had been his; and after he was drafted I wore it every day. For years. How could I have forgotten? I wonder what happened to the original. It probably got too small—as we say, when we mean we've gotten too big—and I gave it away. The jolt comes from the physical memory the jacket gives me of my younger self. All in a flash I am walking on a winter beach, in my twenty-two-year-old body—I have a slow, loose walk, I am in no hurry, it is another world. For a second, I am that young again. Then the phone rings.

A VP named Bill, a real pain in the ass, but you already know that, wants me to pick up some reports he wants copied. On my way to his office, walking past the partitions, I still remember that loose-limbed walk, but I am not walking it.

Bill motions to me to come in when I hesitate outside his open door. He holds the reports up in one hand, he holds the phone in the other, he doesn't look at me or at the phone, he is staring up at the ceiling. "I'm on it," he tells somebody.

I take the reports from his hand and leave. I don't have to turn my head to know that his eyes don't follow me. Nobody's eyes follow me now. Around the time I turned fifty I became invisible. That, for me, was the upside of fifty. As a child I'd wanted to be invisible, and now I am. And of course the best part is that it is a short step from Invisible to Gone.

I like your copying room. It has a window, and while I'm waiting I can look outside, so I do. I am wondering what happened to Ray. I know what happened to him in the ordinary way. I know the woman he married, I know the house they bought in the country when he came home from Vietnam, and the boy they had—who didn't, as we say to one another these days, "turn out." But the Ray I knew, that Ray is as invisible as I am. I suspect *Ray* wouldn't recognize *that* Ray if he met him on the street. Or saw him in the mirror behind the bar he's probably sitting at right now.

I collate forms and put them in stacks. This is the kind of work I like. Tasks. The more repetitive, the duller, the less you value them, the happier I am doing them. What I can't do now is interact. I am not a "team player." But temps don't have to be team players. We just have to "dress appropriately." And show up. As I walk back to Bill's office I see people gathering their belongings, neatening their desks, getting ready to go home. Bill's still on the phone. I put the papers on his desk and leave.

On the bus, it takes an hour to cover the distance I used to drive in twenty minutes. But that's fine with me. I look out the window. I look *down* on people in their cars. They try to squeeze by us, but our bus driver cuts them off with élan, and leaves them in our thick, roiling, black exhaust. They give us the finger, but we're bigger than they are—they can honk, they can flip us the bird, they can do whatever they want, *they still lose.* They may be richer, but we're bigger. There are more of us too, lots of us, riding the bus, crowding the sidewalks, dawdling in the crosswalks, and we scare the people in the cars. In this part of town the people in cars are outnumbered and they know it. Sometimes I can see the fear in their faces. In your face, maybe. More and more I find I enjoy this.

I get off at my stop and start to climb my hill. The hill is steeper now than it was when I moved here, that is to say, it takes me longer to climb it. I lived here for a while when I was young. Then I moved away, now I'm back. Not much has changed, which I like. I've changed of course. I'm invisible now. I'm older. I'm alone. Before, when I lived here, I was young, quite visible, and never alone. I was, in *no* sense of the word, a temp. I was, as they say these days, "fully invested." I was somebody's wife, somebody's mother.

The worst part of motherhood in my estimation, and in total retrospect, is the fact that one is never alone. When my daughter was young a neighbor's little girl called us The LynBeth. My daughter's name was Lyn, and mine was Beth. Because she always saw us together, hand in hand, she thought we were the same creature—the astonishing Lyn-Beth. Her mother, an Australian woman who was married to a painter, told me this; she thought it was cute. I can't say I did. Now I live in a "court-apartment" only half a block from the house I lived in then. I don't know where the Australian woman lives. Australia I suppose. I know she and the painter divorced. That was a foregone conclusion even then. The painter had his hand up my skirt every time his wife went into the kitchen to make a new pot of tea. And I suppose their little girl is middle-aged. Like my daughter. Like you, probably. The whole world is run by middle-aged children now. You're everywhere—managing offices, talking over the radio, listening to our hearts, filling our teeth, even running for Congress.

I'm not sure why I came back here. Of all places. Because I always go back to places, I guess. Try and keep me away. Some have. My cousin, for instance. She got a restraining order to keep me a block away from what she is calling *her* house. In New Orleans. It's not her house, it's my house, our grandmother promised it to me, but try and prove something like that. In court, I mean.

By the time she got the injunction I wasn't even trying to get the house anymore. I just wanted to see it—to smell its smells, to walk through its rooms, memorizing the patterns of its rugs and curtains, but she wouldn't let me in. So I parked my car in front and just sat there looking at the house. I did this for a week. My cousin told the police that she was afraid to go outside for her mail. She had me charged with "stalking." I ask you, how can someone sitting in a blue '83 Nova, chain-smoking mentholated cigarettes, be said to be *stalking* anybody? But she produced some incautious letters I'd written her from the "facility" the same month our grandmother died, and the judge enjoined me from going near the house.

She could have saved herself the trouble and expense, because by the time the papers came through I'd moved on. I had no desire to see her or the house ever again. I had it inside my head. That's why I'd sat out front and looked at it for a week—to get it inside my head. Along with everything else.

Life is so convenient that way. Everything and everyone you've ever known is all stored in one spot, topside—under your expensive cut, your hat, your thin pageboy, your comb-over, your ridiculous ponytail, your backwards baseball cap, whatever you've got up there. You can be transported "Far Beyond the Northern Sea," as the old song my father liked to sing had it, and still leave nothing behind. Everywhere you go, there you are. All of you. Along with everybody you ever knew.

Some years ago my daughter cut me off. She blames me for something that happened. Or that maybe happened. Or never happened at all. Pick one. She thinks that she is punishing me with her absence and her silence. But like my house in New Orleans, I've got my daughter inside my head, and I see her whenever I want. Which, considering the way she's turned out, isn't very often, but at least it is at *my* convenience. My husband doesn't talk to me either, well that can be said of a great many husbands, but mine of course took it to extremes. He could have walked out the door any time, but it never occurred to him, so to make his point he dropped dead. Well, he was a born extremist—politics, art, religion, you name it—it was in his nature to take a thing to its limit—he spent his whole life overboard. Furiously treading water.

I can still see him too. All of the Hims I knew over all the years. It's

like with the Elvis Presley stamp. Remember? Did we want a representation of the young Hound Dog Elvis or the Las Vegas Jump-Suit Elvis?
Being Americans we put it to a vote. In the matter of my husband, I am
a majority of one, and I usually vote for the young husband. The good-
looking, pleasant one. Why not? They say you're only young once, but
that's not quite true—inside other people's heads you'll always be as
young, or as old (also as good or as bad), as they want you to be. Whenever they want you to be it.

"Aren't you lonely?" My old friend Glenda sometimes asks me this
when she phones. She's the only real person who phones now, except
for the girls from the temp agency.

And I say, no. No lonelier, anyway, than I was before. And at least
now I don't have to pretend not to be lonely. (Or, for that matter, that
I don't *like* it.)

I pass the Australian woman's old house. I pass my own old house.
I can still picture us the way we were when we lived there. I can almost believe that if I were to creep up to the window and peek inside, I
would see my husband and Lyn and myself sitting at the supper table.
Having a pleasant family meal. Well, ok, sitting at the supper table.

I walk another half-block up the hill and here is the place I live now.
It has one of my new names on the mailbox. I got tired of my old name,
at about the same time everybody else did; I don't use it anymore. Now
I use the names that I find on the nameplates on the desks where they
put me in the offices I temp in. Like yours. (Your name, by the way, isn't
getting much mail.)

I don't lock my door, well, I can't because I lost the key. Anyway,
there's nothing left to steal. Unless you count books—and thieves, I've
discovered, are not much on books. Too difficult to transport. Still it's
home to me. For the duration.

In all honesty, all I'd really like back from my old life, the one I lived
with my onetime family and my real name, is a dog. I miss dogs. Dogs
don't last in your head in quite the same way that people do. Dogs are
kind of a here and now proposition. Real creature comforts. But as
we've learned, you don't always get what you want.

I go in the kitchen and hang my jacket and bag on the back of a
chair, then I put water on for tea. I stand at the sink and look out my

little window at the doves scrapping in the palm fronds. All the while I'm waiting for the kettle to boil I have the oddest feeling that someone is watching me. When I turn around I see I was right. The old me, the one with the old name, has materialized inside my new-old jacket, and she is sitting in the chair, young and pretty—watching me. Watching to see how I do things now. She will not be, I have good reason to know, particularly charitable.

I snatch the jacket off the chair and hang it in the hall closet and slam the door on it. And her. Back in the kitchen, I turn on the radio. They're talking about the stock market. It's down. Well, one of them is. Yesterday it was up. Or one of them was. As I'm sure *you* know, there are two markets now, with two distinct names. Or is it three? Anyway, one is up and the other is down, or they're both up or they're both down. More and more they're all down. But soar or plummet, it makes exactly zero difference to me. What a relief! For somebody, not anybody in this neighborhood, of course, but maybe you, or that jackass Bill at your office, this stock market news is going to be bad news. Maybe really *bad* news. For me it's just two young men who aren't as bright as they think they are, with annoying verbal mannerisms, talking on the radio. I don't have to listen. No more bad news for me.

Like after I had polio, when I was eight—which I survived with nothing but what my mother always insisted on calling "an imperceptible limp," which required me to wear a rather *perceptible* orthopedic shoe for six years—I alone of all the children I knew could cavort in Lake Pontchartrain during the month of August. I was immunized before there was a vaccine. I'd had the real thing, you see. Just as now. I've had my bad news. All of it. Death's not in it. Not mine, certainly not yours, not anybody's—I've been to the mountain; I've been down in the valley. As Dr. King said, "It doesn't matter to me now."

I can listen to the stock market report; I can watch movies in which dogs and small children die; I can watch men open up their mouths to show us their fake white teeth, and lie—with their hands on any number of Bibles—to the rest of us, and it doesn't matter to me. In the least. I'm no longer in it for the long haul. I am, and I can't stress this too strongly, a temp.

Glenda still gets upset about things. I listen and make the right noises to be polite, because on the rare occasions I actually talk, Glenda listens and makes the right noises. Glenda fires off e-mails to her senators and congressman. "You go, Glenda," I say. And I mean it. People have to do those things while they still can, else we'd be in even deeper than we are now. But it can't be me. Anymore. You want to drill for oil in Yellowstone? Go ahead, bears can *adapt*. You say people need to take responsibility for their own actions? I have done it. That's how I got here. That's why I'm a temp, that's why I live alone in this court apartment, with nothing but a state ID and a bus pass in my wallet, my temp schedule taped to the fridge, and a Banquet TV dinner in a microwave so old it has dials.

But, after I eat my doll-size portion of chicken Parmesan, after I take my bath and iron my "appropriate clothes" and hang them on the shower rod, I can climb into my bed and get down to it—the real business of my day. I can sort through all the people I keep in my head, and choose someone, not just any old someone, the exact *right* somebody for this exact moment in time (*my* time) to dream about. My young husband maybe, or tonight, for old time's sake, Ray, or my grandmother, or my best friend Susie O'Delle from sixth grade, who knows, I could even pluck Lyn from her well-deserved obscurity for one night! And I'll place them in the exact right seasons and houses and landscapes, and dream about them all night long. Doing and saying things I want them to do and say. And they will see me as I want to be seen—young and pretty and, most of all, *kind*. Kindness is very important, don't you think? It is to me.

And at night and in dreams, time makes all its old sense again, which is a great relief, since during the day I can't help but hear the awful racket it makes in passing. It makes this really bad ratcheting sound. You've heard it. A close approximation anyway. Remember when you saw that lady parking cop, the one with the too tight trousers, and the really fat butt, standing by your car, pad in hand, and you raced up—because you knew you had at least three minutes left, *five*, maybe—and you got there just in time to hear that funny whirring sound, followed by the resounding *clunk* a parking meter makes at the exact moment its red flag whips up—and you stood there, and you heard that sound, and you looked the cop in her squinty, squinty eye, and you knew that you were really, really, *fucked*? See? You *have* heard it.

Well, should I decide to wake up again tomorrow morning, and I may not, because, remember, I am a temp, but *if* I should wake up, thanks to you, I will have somebody to be and someplace to go.

I will walk down my hill, and catch a big, belching bus, with gang signs scribbled across its flanks, to your office, where I will be you. Where I will pass the time, sitting at your desk, opening your mail, looking at the picture of your daughter, answering your phone, and, yes, using your name. I may be the luckiest woman in the world. But of course, and for obvious reasons, that's entirely up to you. So, and I really *mean* this, Good Luck!

AMY NEWMAN
The Cat

The old cat turns by curving
what's left of his body
beyond the careless trees. Does it ache,

each twinge and cramp, to wander in hunger,
ever fruitless at eye level?
Across the lawn the sunlight has nearly given up

dragging out its whites like a chapel veil,
faking away its sullied past,
having come all that way to promise tenderness

only to flee again, leaving me, my mouth, my heart.
Now the deadpan fox has changed his course.
The twitch and bristle of instinct,

tender as murder, my god, and next,
under the mangy strands of wind, under the chill,
animals are sources, little meats!

Let the loving deaths begin,
let out the ashes, the brocade of bone,
layer atop layer of flesh unfastened,

the veins undone, the whole skinflint world.
Aren't you tired of it all, aren't you weary,
cat, having to place one foot after the other

toward evening's stingy gristle? No comment.
Neither the cat nor the grass he bothers
can recognize any largeness of his life,

the creature's stubborn desire
to find its commonplace, its eternal,
as if anything ever adds up to poetry.

The sun's gone now. Bleak forfeit.
Old habits pacing, the wind rearranging its *yes*.
x-ray moon on the evening's bones, revising.

AMY NEWMAN

Making Small Talk, the Cashier at the Grocery Store Inadvertently Creates a Religion

Passing the pears over the electronic scanner, she says
These are beautiful. Look at the markings!
And: *I don't know the story of where they're from.*
But I believe they are just right.
And passing the figs:
So complex, what's on the inside.
Everything worthwhile has a kind of mystery.
I don't bother with it more than that.
The chèvre in its paper, rolled
and taped, she handles with care.
I'll put that on top. With delicate things
it's best to be careful. What is it?
she asks. When I tell her goat cheese,
she smiles. *Everything,* she says,
that partakes of the grasses
will taste of the grasses. Everything
that partakes of the earth...
and in all this rain we've been having...
passing the berries across,
waving the delicate wafers by the scanning eye.
I just let the day unfold, she says
waving the bottle of wine across,
and try to dress accordingly.

D. NURKSE
1967

1

I was hired to finish interiors in Cloverdale
but I didn't know how: how to pry open
the zinc-tabbed five-gallon tub: how
to slide out the balsa paddle without leaving
a maze of white dots on oak parquet:
how deep and long to dip the bristle:
perhaps it was a problem of language: *paint*
was verb or noun or both or neither.
So I watched Mr. Colraine and Mr. Emil Toxer
but saw no common measure. Mr. Colraine
wiggled a sash brush and attacked the wall
with wide looping inward-concentric gestures
which melded as an image forms in the retina
but into blankness. Mr. Emil Toxer
knelt and inched along the molding,
crept back to his starting point, finished
five hours early, lit a Parodi, and poured himself
six ounces of Sneaky Pete from a pint stashed
in an empty stain vat. At sunset I drove home

2

through the projects, passing those small parks
where collies run canted as their frisbees tilt,
where the swing stands at apogee and a child
spits on her hands, enters the jump rope eye
and sings herself to twilight.

3

I came to your house, dusted the narrow chime
with my cuff, realigned the two ashcans

so the crenellated one showed its best profile,
and entered your level eyes like a minnow
darting into Lake Michigan. I didn't know
how to be naked. I imagined Mr. Colraine
in his four layers of spackle-stiff mesh v-shirts
and Mr. Emil Toxer who never spilled a drop.

All I knew was: each act had a past and future,
an almost and an absolute, but the present
was just a cry, then a soft gliding return
to a dim room with a jar of Vaseline,
a votive candle, and a peony in a wineglass.

I realized almost immediately that the task
was to wait for dawn and your Manx cat
was practicing, narrowing her green stare
in anticipation of sunrise, so I followed
her light quick breaths, and here I am.

D. NURKSE
The Surface

The sandhogs who blasted the Lincoln Tunnel
jerry-rigged an escarpment a quarter-mile down
but it buckled at riptide and one journeyman
was sucked into the air pocket, up through the lattice,
through the ooze under the Hudson, to surface
in daylight—how the hell did he remember
to drop his ninety pound jute sack and let himself float
until a tug lowered a skiff—now no one knows his name—

Mr. Modesto in for his second hernia told this story
in the waiting room behind the nurses' station
at Downstate—view of a gasworks, Szechuan takeout,
cat hunting a spindled leaf, laundry on tenement roofs,
three clouds, one bright, one tinged, one darkening.

Mr. Solaris, like me a recent father, nodded sleepily,
scratching his head and mechanically rolling the dead skin
between thumb and forefinger, perhaps to release the odor.

But Mrs. Hiram Q. Pace, whose brother had Alzheimer's,
never looked up from her sudoku and the nameless man
in the seersucker suit with the hairline rip at one elbow,
who had never spoken since the beginning, swept up his Patience
to reshuffle—how could he shuffle for himself—
so the cards hung luminous between his hands

when the nurse in the corridor cleared her throat
and we each looked up with a question on our lips
but I was the one the crooked finger summoned
to kneel by my wife and hold my breathing child.

REBECCA OKRENT
Gratified Desire

If you lifted the "house" from "housewife"
it would not be such a bad job,
not partnered to rooms or dust,
but to the man,
the small burden of laughing
at repeated jokes.

Who wouldn't admire
the woman's shining competence at love
and accommodation?
The lineaments of practiced ardor?
Yes, there's abnegation,
but wife burns.

Enough to set the house on fire.

REBECCA OKRENT
Star Sapphire

What might it be worth, this memento
of my parents' fifty-year marriage set
in a diamond and sapphire crown, too large,
too gaudy for my taste?
I pass it under the partition
to the jeweler who holds it to the light,
then under the stern eye of his loupe.

(Do you see it, young man? The doctor
asks the consumptive as,
floor pulsing, light snapping,
he stares at the fluoroscope image,
into the skeletal chamber of his cousin's
aquatic heart.) The gemstone

might have been mined in Burma or Ceylon.
The jeweler's sad eyes return to me,
pronounce the fraud: Synthetic. Union
Carbide 1940s. Thirty dollars. Sorry.
It's not the wad of bills I regret but the story,
the jewel worth risking a life for, hidden in a bodice

during border crossings. I want
the fedora-topped ancestor killed by a trolley in Moscow,
a shard of unyielding amber in his pocket,
not the Huguenot pioneer felled by a tree on the plains,
the ring supposed to have only sentimental value
until hard times force the lone survivor to sell—

worth more than anyone imagined.

LINDA PASTAN
Anatomy

In the tenement
of the body
generations have left
their mark.

On the stairwell
of bones and the
walls of flesh
illegible words

are scrawled
in invisible ink.
Windows look down
on concrete gardens

where live buds
force themselves
from sticks
of trees.

The genes are doing
their scheduled work.
Clutch the banister,
hold on tight.

LINDA PASTAN
Pastoral

Every garden dreams
of being Eden: rosebushes
or wildflowers, it hardly matters
as long as the hum of bees
remains peaceable and the door
to the grave stays hidden
beneath a swath of grass.
In the cooling afternoon
each flower relaxes
on its pedestal of stem,
and the gardener too dreams,
under a tree weighted
each fall with apples.

LINDA PASTAN
Traveling Light

I'm only leaving you
for a handful of days,
but it feels as though
I'll be gone forever—
the way the door closes

behind me with such solidity,
the way my suitcase
carries everything
I'd need for an eternity
of traveling light.

I've left my hotel number
on your desk, instructions
about the dog
and heating dinner. But
like the weather front

they warn is on its way
with its switchblades
of wind and ice,
our lives have minds
of their own.

Marriage, East Berlin

I.

It came in like a quiet boat at night.
We still don't know who sent it
or why. Some days it makes us shake.

We kept on cooking for each other
and bathing ourselves.
We looked at children
but the music of Chopin
always replaced the sight of them.

In its coming, it took away.
Over the years we grew
to understand that we were losing
our hold on each other
even though at night we would
send the gift of one thought
back and forth,
I'm here for you if you need me—

Back and forth,
in our sleep.

I'm here even if you don't.

II.

When the wall came down
we went in the other direction.

It was not freedom we wanted,
but to be tied forever to a man
in a room, through a wiretap,
listening to the sound of our breathing
and reporting back to his superior
that we ached for basic things:
our fathers, a baby,
and a way to understand
how to exit this life
without each other.

SCOTT NADELSON
Dolph Schayes's Broken Arm

The summer I first discovered how it feels to suffer in love, I worked for a local newspaper, selling subscriptions over the phone. It was a miserable job, and I was lousy at it. I stumbled through my script, apologizing too often, agreeing with people on the other end of the line that it was rude to call during dinner, that the paper wasn't well-written, that no one needed so much recycling to haul out to the curb every week. Occasionally I'd convince some grandma hard of hearing to sign up for a trial subscription, free for two weeks, failing to mention that the subscription would continue past the trial period if she didn't call to cancel. I sold one daily to a thirteen-year-old, whose father later threatened to sue the company. The job paid minimum wage plus commission. Some of my co-workers made upwards of twenty bucks an hour. Most weeks I put in forty hours and took home less than $180.

I was twenty years old, just finished with my junior year of college, and the previous semester I'd spent in the bed of a girl who'd marked me in a way I now recognize. I wish there were adequate words to describe this sort of thing. The best I can manage is to say that she'd moved something inside me, as if her touch had rearranged my organs. I've experienced the feeling again from time to time, but then it was entirely new and left me in pain even before we'd separated for the summer, she to her parents' house on the south shore of Long Island, me to my parents' in north central New Jersey. The real pain, though, started only when I made it home. The girl—I'll call her Kara—took a day or two to return my calls, and when we did talk, there was a distance in her voice I didn't want to admit to. She put off making plans to visit, talking instead about all the old friends with whom she'd reconnected, all the parties to which she'd been invited. One name—Darren, I think—came up too frequently. I pretended not to hear it. She told me about going, on a whim, to a psychic, who'd told her she had all sorts of adventures ahead of her before she settled down. Adventures sounded fun, I said. We could go on one together. Did she want me to drive out to the Island to see her this weekend? She'd check her schedule, she said, and get back to me.

I don't blame her for any of this. I was young and uncommunicative, she was whimsical and self-involved, and I can see now that by the end of the semester my mooning over her must have become oppressive. We were just kids, and our relationship was brief and trivial and fumbling, and I'm sure she's forgotten me long since. I might have forgotten her too, if not for the suffering she caused me, which didn't feel trivial at all, not then. Not now, either, in part because I've experienced similar suffering since, and its accumulation, I have to believe, accounts at least somewhat for the way I've lived my life, with the expectation that joy will always be tempered by deprivation or longing or loss.

The pain then was physical, located just beneath the arch of my lowest ribs. It was anxiety, I suppose, that wrenched my insides. For most of that summer I couldn't eat without afterward running to the bathroom, sitting hunched in agony as love scoured my bowels. I'd always been slim, and by mid-June, after dropping five pounds, my face looked gaunt, my eyes and cheeks sunken.

At work I didn't eat at all, for fear of embarrassing myself by running out in the middle of a call, and this is likely what kept me from getting fired. At the beginning and end of the dinner break my supervisor saw me sitting at my station, dialing numbers—the paper didn't have money for automated dialers, or headsets, for that matter—and must have decided I was motivated, if not competent. My coworkers might have begun to resent me, an overachiever, if my commission didn't stay flat from one week to the next. Instead they gave me pep talks, assuring me that when they'd started they'd averaged only four or five subscriptions a week. They were kind not to point out that my average was one and a half.

I didn't actually make any calls during the dinner break, instead keeping my finger on the receiver button as I dialed, running through my pitch to customers who didn't exist. It was disconcerting to hear my voice alone in the call room, stammering, apologizing, blowing even imaginary sales. When the others were there, my voice was lost in a chorus of aggressive hustling, and it was easier to forget how awkward I sounded, to imagine I was part of a team that was accomplishing something, even if I contributed nothing. My coworkers' sales invigorated me, and I listened to their calls with a measure of hope, a hand pressed to my aching middle.

One voice always stood out from the rest. It belonged to Stanley Davidson, a broad, well-dressed man in his late sixties, the only person to come to work in a jacket and tie. The other men, including myself, wore jeans and T-shirts, and some of the women came in sweats. Most of us ran through our scripts as fast as possible, hoping to ambush potential customers into signing up out of sheer bewilderment. Stanley spoke slowly, carefully, enunciating every word. He detailed the merits of *The Daily Record*, from its thorough coverage of local high school sports to its comic strips for children and adults—his grandkids loved *Peanuts*, he'd say, and he never missed *Doonesbury*—including the reams of coupons on Sunday. "My wife saved nearly $200 last week at the Pathmark. That's no small chunk of change." Whether he made a sale or not, he always ended his calls by saying, "I do thank you for your time, sir, and wish you a pleasant evening." As far as I could tell, no one ever hung up on him.

At first I thought Stanley was simply indifferent to his commission, as I was trying to be, but when I sat next to him during a shift and peeked around the divider that separated our stations, I quickly discovered this wasn't true. When he hung up the phone, he'd respond in one of two ways. If he'd sold a subscription he'd raise his hands over his head and toss an invisible ball toward an invisible rim, catching, I imagined, nothing but net. But if the call went badly he'd curse under his breath, bounce a fist softly on his desk, and then say, louder, in his deep, calm, salesman's voice, "Easy, Stanley." Unlike the others in the call room, he never offered me any advice or encouragement, but after overhearing me flub four calls in a row, he stuck his head around the divider and said, "No need to be so nervous. We aren't selling warheads, last I checked."

"Maybe I should start reading the paper," I said. "If I knew it as well as you do—"

"I wouldn't use it to wipe my ass," he said. "Not even if it was wrapped in silk."

When I asked how long he'd been working at the *Record*, he glared at me, his face too narrow for its length, I thought, as if his skull had been pinched in a vice, his nose a pitted blotch in its center, eyes heavily hooded. After a moment he said, firmly, "If I don't work, I drink."

The safest subject to approach with Stanley, I soon found out, was basketball, which he'd played in the schoolyards of the Bronx as a teenager, alongside the great Dolph Schayes. I'd never heard of Dolph Schayes but gave an impressed nod anyway, and then looked him up when I got home. "He'd still be the best player in the league," Stanley said, "even with all these big shines and their slam dunks. The man knew how to pass." Stanley and I were both Knicks fans, and this season—1993–94—was the most promising we'd had since I was old enough to watch. Our star center, Patrick Ewing, was getting old for the game, and his knees were fragile. Before they gave out, we had one last chance to come away with a championship. Stanley brought a little transistor radio to work, one he must have had for the past twenty years, with a single flesh-colored plug he'd slip into his left ear when our supervisor was out of the room. Between calls he'd lean around our divider and update me on games in progress, giving more detail than I needed—not just who'd scored but who'd taken down rebounds or made steals and assists. "It's all about passing," he said whenever the Knicks blew an offensive possession. "That's what these people don't understand. Pass, pass, pass. And always keep moving. No one should ever be standing still."

That year, the Knickerbockers—Stanley always called them by their full name—were tough, scrappy underdogs, strong on defense, and even if I hadn't grown up rooting for them, I would have admired them now. Their roughness appealed to me, their ability to come from behind and squeak out improbable victories. Those evenings I wasn't working I watched every game, hunched forward on my parents' couch to take pressure off my tortured insides. Not quite consciously, I'd begun to pin my hopes on the feisty Knicks, believing that my fortunes were tied up with theirs. The hazy superstition took on real shape after they won the first round of the playoffs, beating the Nets in four games. Kara called a few minutes later, sounding cheerful, pleased to hear my voice. She wasn't a fan, didn't watch sports at all, but still I took it as a sign. I didn't talk to her about basketball, except to mention what I was doing with my free nights, and she couldn't talk long anyway. She was heading out with friends. I didn't ask which friends, but she told me anyway—Melissa, Jamie, Darren.

The rest of the playoffs were agonizing. Both the conference semifinals and finals went to seven games, with the Knicks just barely scraping out enough wins to advance to the championship series. After a loss I was in such pain and so agitated that I couldn't sit still, and even if it was close to midnight I'd head out into my parents' quiet neighborhood, the neighborhood in which I'd spent a simple, placid childhood, and run feverish laps around the block. Some nights I sat on the toilet, doubled up in a cold sweat, until after dawn.

That Stanley, too, was tormented by the Knicks made me feel close to him. We were in this together. A championship was a matter of life and death. Those days following a loss, he looked as if he hadn't slept any more than I had, his blazer rumpled, his face puffy. "Flat-footed," he'd say. "No one wins without moving and passing."

During the championship series he could hardly work. He sat hunched over his phone, hands cupped over his ears to hide his earplug, making calls only during timeouts and commercial breaks. Our supervisor couldn't have failed to notice, but she let it go. And in any case, even making just a few calls an hour, Stanley still sold four times as many subscriptions as I did. For their part, the Knicks seemed outmatched. They lost two of the first three games, Patrick Ewing's height countered by that of Houston's star center, Hakeem Olajuwon. "Dolph could have beat either of them," Stanley said. "I don't care how tall they are."

When the series came home to Madison Square Garden, Stanley took two nights off from work. A friend had tickets to the games, all the way up in the last row of the blue seats, the very top of the arena, but he wouldn't miss this chance for anything. "I didn't make it in '73," he said. "You don't let history pass you by twice, right?" I was born in '73, and had the feeling that history had passed me by altogether, but I agreed with Stanley and told him to cheer extra loud for me. He lent me his radio, with the pink earplug, and for those two nights I suffered alone, imagining Stanley saying, "Pass, pass, move, move!" while I stumbled through my awkward sales pitch, telling people who'd probably never read a newspaper in their lives how much they could save off the news-stand price. At times the pain in my guts made me close my eyes. When the Knicks were down I was nearly in tears. But against all odds they pulled out wins both nights. One more, and they'd be champs.

When I came home after the second night, there was a message waiting for me from Kara, her voice on my parents' answering machine warmer than I'd heard it since we'd left campus in early May. She missed me, she said, and hoped we could find a time to visit soon.

Stanley came to work the next evening looking dapper and composed, though there was something manic in his smile and the way he slapped my back and said, "Did you see how they were moving?" I didn't bother reminding him that I'd listened to the game on his radio and couldn't have seen anything. "Just like Dolph and me. Never take a shot without first looking to pass." His calls that night were manic too, his pitch hastier than usual, some of his words slurred. Whether he made a sale or not he raised his hands and tossed his invisible ball into its invisible net. When we broke for dinner he pulled me out of my chair. "Come and eat," he said. "You're practically skeletal." I tried to make an excuse, saying I didn't have any money for dinner, that I needed to keep making calls to boost my commission. "Face it, kid," he said. "You're not making any more money until you get a new job. And anyway, I'm buying."

I followed him out of the call center, but instead of heading into the break room, he led me outside, down to the parking lot. He popped the trunk on a huge silver Lincoln, recently washed and waxed, and pulled out a pair of deli sandwiches and bags of potato chips. I was touched that he'd have thought of me when he stopped at the deli, but my mouth was so unused to food that the roast beef tasted burnt to me, its texture slick and heavy and hard to swallow.

He reached into the trunk again, and only now, as he brought out a pair of plastic cups and a half-gallon bottle of gin, did I understand his sloppy smile and slurred speech. "Two more games, and all we need is one win," he said, handing me a cup and pouring generously. "Sometimes you've got to celebrate along the way." I took a few sips and then stopped, waiting to see if the booze would loosen the knot inside me or yank it tighter. It was a warm night, and we were close enough to the freeway to hear trucks roaring east toward Long Island, or west away from the girl I loved. Stanley downed his cup and refilled it. Because I had nothing else to say, I asked him about playing with Dolph Schayes, whose record I now knew almost by heart, from his college days at NYU to his championship season with the Syracuse Nationals in 1955. Stanley set down his cup on the Lincoln's roof. He dribbled an invisible ball, spun, passed, cut across the parking lot, and made a slow but surprisingly graceful layup. He came back breathing hard, stepping gingerly with his right foot.

"He was better than most people give him credit for," he said, "and most people say he was one of the best ever. He was *the* best ever. Not even a question. When I played with him he was good, and then he broke his arm and got even better. Can you imagine, playing a whole season with a broken arm? His *shooting* arm, for Godsakes. He didn't sit on the bench like one of these big pansy shines. Played the whole time. Learned to shoot lefty. Can you imagine? Not even Mr. Tongue-Wagger Jordan could do something like that."

He took another shot, this one lazy and half-hearted, and then picked up his cup. He drained it and filled it again. "I was pretty good too," he said. "Not like Dolph—no one was. But I wasn't bad. Baseline shot, that was my specialty. But nine times out of ten I'd pass. I wasn't selfish, not like these ball-hogs today." He could have gone on to play college ball, he said. He'd gotten an offer, not from a big-shot program, like NYU, but some place in Ohio, a school he'd never heard of. But that was in late '44, and the war was on. As soon as he was eighteen he signed up. He'd just shipped out of San Diego, a few hundred miles into the Pacific, when the bomb fell on Hiroshima. "It was all over by the time I got there."

He said it sadly, as if this were the great disappointment in his life, much worse than working a terrible job selling newspapers in order to keep himself from drinking. He drank now, another long gulp, and I handed him the second half of my sandwich. He finished it without a word. He looked rumpled again, his blazer sagging on his shoulders. My bowels churned, and even though we had another fifteen minutes before the break was over, I had to excuse myself and run for the bathroom. I was glad to get away from him, from the images he'd put in my mind, of Dolph Schayes playing ball with a broken arm, of a young man on the deck of a ship, yearning for a war that was over before he could join it. Both things added to the weight inside me, to the small glimmer of hope that grew more painful with every passing day, with every feat of Patrick Ewing and his small band of scrappy underdogs. I told myself I'd never eat again.

When I came back from the bathroom, empty and sweating, Stanley was at his station, leaning back in his chair, eyes closed. I spent the rest of the shift with my finger on the receiver button, pretending to dial, running through my script more fluently than ever, offering huge savings to people who weren't there.

The Knicks, of course, lost the series. The sixth game was a heartbreaker, close until the final moments. I watched the seventh on my day off, alone, in agony, imagining that my appendix had burst. The next day, Stanley and I didn't talk. He sat morosely in his station, making calls in his old, calm, steady voice, racking up sales, raising his commission. I wanted him to comfort me, to say that our Knickerbockers would be back next year, a stronger team, with more experience. I wanted him to tell me that Ewing still had a few good years left in his knees. Kara hadn't returned my most recent call, and by now I was mostly certain she wouldn't, except to let me know that she'd met someone else, that she was sorry to hurt me, that I was a great guy who was certain to make some lucky girl happy, that her psychic had told her so.

That call did come, eventually, at the end of the summer, long after I'd lost the job at the newspaper and found a better one at a screen printing shop, where I hosed off squeegees and folded t-shirts and ducked behind the building with my coworkers to smoke joints two or three times a day. By then my appetite had returned—helped by the joints, I'm sure—and I even found myself interested in another girl, the shop's shy receptionist. I slept with her before the summer was over and then didn't call her, as I promised I would, when I went back to school in the fall.

But that day after the Knicks' defeat, I couldn't have imagined any of this. I still had a tiny nugget of hope buried in a heap of despair, and the pain inside me was unbearable. I'd given up making calls altogether and was beginning to catch looks from my supervisor, whose compassion, I knew, would extend only so far. It unnerved me that Stanley's voice was so calm and assured, betraying nothing. Toward the end of the shift I peeked around the divider, and then I could see what his words didn't let on. After he logged a subscription, he just went on to the next call without shooting a hoop. And when he blew an easy sale, his fist pounded the desk. Then he picked up the receiver and clocked himself, hard, across the temple. Hard enough to make him wince and grunt and close his eyes.

Somehow it was the worst thing I'd ever seen, and I wished I hadn't seen it at all. That life could turn out to be so disappointing was excruciating enough, but watching someone add willingly to his own pain was too much for me. My own eyes burned with threatening tears, and I turned my chair away. I wanted to tell Stanley something, but what could I say? That not everyone could be as good as Dolph? That for most people it was pointless to play ball with a broken arm? That he should have felt lucky to have missed the war and all its dangers, the likelihood that he wouldn't have survived?

When our shift ended, the supervisor asked me to stay behind. I said goodbye to Stanley, knowing I wouldn't see him again. He only muttered, "Another day, another dollar lost for you," and brushed past me. I imagined I saw a lump rising on his forehead. I kept picturing it as I drove away, growing larger and purple, spreading across his receding hairline, and wondered how he'd explain it to his wife when he got home, to his coworkers when he returned in the morning. The sky had turned that same shade of purple, the whole world become an enormous, tender bruise. By the time I made it to my parents' house, the noose around my guts had loosened the slightest bit, and I knew I no longer had hope for anything.

KATHA POLLITT

Angels

They thought the job would be more musical:
Rainbows and trumpets. They'd burst
through clouds of marble streaked with flame

and offer blinding demonstrations
of the ontological proof of God.
People would look up and say "Ineffable!"

Instead, they swooped through the mall
calling *Ashley? Pammy?*
fished Mrs. Baines' wedding ring from the drain *again*,

and suspended the laws of physics on the freeway,
while simultaneously fielding the collective pleas
of Sister Perpetua's seventh grade:

Bauxite, they hiss. *Cortez. Tegucigalpa.*
Why don't they just study? one angel would gripe to another,
She *told* them Latin America would be on the test.

Gradually, they stopped showing up.
They moved into studio apartments
and took day jobs working with plants and animals.

You can spot a pair of them sometimes
at the back of the Greek diner,
giggling and whispering over fruit plates:

No, Timmy, really:
The principle export of Bolivia is lightning.
Or maybe they saunter downtown

at the end of the day, one jingling your keys, the other
tossing your lottery tickets into the gutter.
Later they'll find their way to the dark little bar

hidden away below decks,
order cocktails named after movie stars
and try out the bed in your stateroom

on a liner that left exactly on time, after all.

CHELSEA RATHBURN
Sweet Nothings

After gimlets and cosmopolitans,
we're on to sex and its catastrophes,
Susan telling about the time she ordered
a paycheck's worth of Italian lingerie.
She dressed slowly, she says, feeling only
a little ridiculous as she slid
one gartered leg across the coffee table.
Looking up, her husband asked if she could stop
blocking the TV. Blushing, Nancy reveals
how she whispered "filthy things"—she won't say what—
into a boyfriend's ear at a boring party,
and he pretended to have been struck deaf.
We find that the old wounds feel a little softer
with a laugh track, so the stories keep coming,
our urge to talk as primal as sex itself.
Then Laura says that she can top us all:
in grad school, she worked as a dominatrix.
Easy money, she says, no sex, just power,
and when we hear her hourly, we're wondering why
we aren't all wielding whips and riding boots,
until she arrives at how she lost the job.
It is the middle of the afternoon,
and in a downtown loft she is handed a mouse.
"He wanted me to kill it as he came,"
she says. "I told him sexuality
can't trump a life, and he said he owned me
for the hour—they only play at giving up
control." There is no bitterness in her voice,
no laughter either. It hangs there, a small warmth
beating in the dark, her story joining
the ones we've told and the ones that we can't tell.

And who among us will feel most naked
in the morning, having sacrificed lovers
or selves to the narrative arc? We split the check,
and no one asks what happened to the mouse.

ERIC RAWSON
Hotel Razing

Snow falls the tenants gather at the corner
Gone are their small poor lives we envy in
The lyrical vein the snow falls as thick

As soap over the monuments over
The benches and the scratched branches the pile
Of tires in the median strip the snow

Falls like excess paperwork on the street-
Lamps and the old-fashioned powerlines on
The discouraged lady singer heading

To work the snow falls the way a species
Goes extinct slowly and thickly coating
The sky with its twenty million pieces

The police come to quell the disturbance
And the snow covers their coats and hats in
Great white bandages the wrecking ball swings

Through the snow the one last candle's little
Angel head glowing through the snow the shrieks
Of a little girl who doesn't know how

To behave during moments of beauty
Only somewhat muffled by the snow and
Then as the building crashes down like a storm

On a hamlet the tenants drift away
Leaving their nice new footprints in the snow

JAY ROGOFF
Swanilda Meets Her Twin

Coppélia

What does it mean? What can it mean? A man
so lonely he goes mad and builds a girl
furnished with everything, and yes, I mean
everything. Just look: right down to the curl
of our disputed provinces, she's my twin,
Alsace to my Lorraine, no blood but oil
for beaus who blanch, or stick at human friction.
And her eyes, miracles of darkened vision,

glow tough and glossy, unlike mine—enamel
like a tooth: I can tap them with my fingers,
click click like a machine. Mine can't dissemble
so well, though Franz ensures they're washed with tears.
He stares upon her stupid stare as simple
as a china plate, moaning and mooing. She bears
nothing but genius, reflection of rejection,
shining eyes repulsive in attraction.

Even if your face gets slapped,
or fingers probe you, read your book.
I have made you. You can't decay.
When my life work lies full revealed,

damn the goose girls giggling round
my steps through town. Come, life's delight:
joy in your drop-dead china eyes,
stone silence from your dead heart.

NICHOLAS SAMARAS
Crashing Slow and Sudden

What I also didn't expect was the premonition.
Through the windshield, I half-saw two angels, two
somber old gentlemen telling me my life was due.

But when I thought to them I still have
a five-year-old son to raise, and asked to be given
the time to raise him, they both stepped

back from me in my head. At that exact second,
the speeding right front tire ripped off our car entirely,
my daughter and son screaming from the back seats.

Our whole car floated across three highway lanes,
threaded through huge blocks of titan trucks. Smashed
down into the asphalt, we still floated to rest perfectly

in the breakdown lane, facing forward. Whole. No sound.
No fire. No flip-over. Just the bizarre and lofty
carrying across the Christmas Day highway that left

our entire family—wife, children, grandparents—
hushed and hovered, a presence there with us,
the sparks and sharded metal and the earth settling.

JOYCE CAROL OATES
Distance

"Ma'am? You can't open the windows, sorry."

Coolly she turned to the boy. Prissy Mexican kid, wearing white-boy wire-rim glasses, who'd brought up her single lightweight suitcase she'd have preferred to have brought herself, to save a tip. But at the hotel check-in downstairs the suave, brisk young woman behind the counter had finessed Kathryn, handing the card key to the bellboy, with no chance for Kathryn to intervene.

"'Can't open the windows'—why not?"

Evasively the boy mumbled what sounded like *sealed.*

"The windows are 'sealed'? But why?"

Kathryn's voice betrayed surprise, dismay. A room in which other occupants had slept recently—their odors left behind, faintly disguised by disinfectant, room "freshener"—was not the ideal setting, for what she anticipated.

Asking again, "Why?"—but the bellboy ignored her. Adjusting a wall thermostat, a rush of air conditioning from overhead. In his pose of concentration there was a mild rebuke, Kathryn thought. A warning, *Don't be ridiculous. Don't ask questions if you don't know the answers. Sealed windows in high-rise hotels in Vegas, you can figure.*

On the third day she called L——.

She would have said *I am testing distance.* Two thousand two hundred thirty-seven miles and three hours separating them.

Except she'd left his telephone number behind. Or she'd lost his telephone number. She'd been hurried packing for her trip and careless, as frequently she was careless in small matters despite her wish to be otherwise—seeing now with a stab of dismay clothes, toiletries, papers scattered across the unused hotel twin bed, where she'd unzipped her suitcase and shaken it in search of the slip of paper she was sure she'd brought with her—she'd meant to bring with her—bearing such crucial phone numbers as his.

What did it mean, she hadn't memorized his telephone number.

What did it mean, she didn't know the man's middle name—not even his middle initial! She wasn't sure of the precise name of the road he lived on, though she'd been brought to his house—by him—several times, and in her mind's eye she could make that journey along that suburban-rural road again at a distance of two thousand two hundred thirty-seven miles and three hours. Thinking, *I can't be sure, I don't know. None of it has entered that deeply into me.*

It was her decision then, to call *directory assistance* for his number. In fact, it was *nationwide directory assistance. City and state please?*

Calling information for his number wasn't identical with calling him of course. Maybe she wouldn't call him. There was that option, purely hers.

Still, it seemed urgent to her—she could not have said why—to have his telephone number written hastily in ballpoint on a notepad on the bedside table of this hotel room at the edge of the desert two thousand two hundred thirty-seven miles and three hours distant from him. Whether she made use of this number or not. *It's in my power. My choice.*

At the other end of the line a (female) recorded voice in a neutral tone neither warmly engaging nor coolly disapproving provided her with a number, which was presumably his number—how quickly it was summoned, before she'd been fully prepared—and this number, when punched into the phone receiver with the brash optimism of a child playing at a game warned to be slightly dangerous, maybe more than just slightly forbidden and for this reason irresistible, triggered a brief spate of ringing, presumably two thousand two hundred thirty-seven miles away, and a *click!* and a (male) recorded voice, *This is the L—— residence. No one can come to the phone at the present time, so please leave a detailed message and you will be called back.* This confused her, stymied her, for her lover lived alone—didn't he? Or had someone else lived with him until recently, and he hadn't gotten around to changing the recording? The voice wasn't precisely her lover's voice but resembled it to a degree to lure her into leaving a message, even as a part of her mind remained skeptical, *This can't be him, such formality isn't like him.* Yet once embarked upon the brief message, she could not break it off—feeling like a fool—so stupid!—embarrassing!—leaving a message in a breathy faltering voice like air leaking from a balloon.

She thought, *Enough! He will never know.*

In fact, it was a relief to think—to assume—that whoever received the message would simply erase it as a wrong number. For surely—she was certain—that formal oldish voice hadn't been her lover's voice. Whatever voice was her lover's voice—she could not recall, just now. In any case, her lover would never hear the message she'd left exposing herself so unambiguously—now she was thinking, with a thrill of euphoria, *why call him at all?* Where was the need to call him? Where was the need to attach herself to *him?*—she was more than two thousand miles away; the man could not touch her and render her weak, unnerved, frantic with sexual desire, nor could she have touched this man had she wanted to touch him. His body, which seemed to her of the weight and density of clayey earth, smelling of damp, of leaves, of the sweetest sort of rot. The taste of her own body in his mouth and his mouth in hers as they lay together like swimmers who have drowned together clutching each other, thrown at last upon a desolate littered shore, and high overhead the figures of long-winged shrieking birds... What need had she of *him!* She disliked him. She hated him. He had hurt her, her body was bruised. He'd laughed hurting her. She had scoured his shoulders and back with scratches, he'd laughed seeing blood on the sheets. She hated him, such intimacy. It was an insult to her, such intimacy. All that—the life of *feeling*—she would have liked to squeeze from her veins drop by drop.

It was so: her soul was of no more substance than the shadows of long-winged birds—a western species of hawk? gull?—eagle?—across the drawn blind of her hotel room window. With a cruel smile she thought, *I will never call him. Never speak with him again.*

In this way she would end it between them, this morning. This was within her power.

As in the east, he was three hours into the morning and for her it wasn't yet dawn.

There was such pleasure in heedlessness, as in cruelty! Eagerly she opened the blind. Pushed aside the drapes that were made of a heavy synthetic fabric. It was exhilarating to her to see that the sun was only just rising at the mountainous horizon. That in every direction she could see, beyond the sprawl of the city, there was an open lunar landscape, unnameable. She thought, *He has no idea where I am, he will never know.*

As he would never know how she'd been awake much of the night as she'd been awake much of the two previous nights. How she resented him, that she'd been awake on his account. Despite the air conditioning, she'd sweated through her nightclothes, and the nape of her neck was damp and sticky and the places he'd touched her were bruised and sore and her mouth still swollen and the fleshy lips between her legs swollen and singular and perverse with their own little heartbeat. *He will never know. No more!*

Yet—so strangely—even as she was thinking she would not call him, that she would tear into shreds the slip of paper with his number on it, that she wouldn't be tempted to call him at a later time, she'd lifted the receiver of the bedside phone and got an outside line and another time consulted *directory assistance* and another time a (female) recorded voice came on. This time she made a point of providing both her lover's name and the name of the street on which he lived in that city two thousand two hundred thirty-seven miles away and three hours into the future so that there could be no chance of a second mistake—previously she'd given just her lover's name. And now she was provided with a number that seemed familiar to her—at least, the first three digits seemed familiar—and this number she called without giving herself time to think *No! no, why are you doing this, you should not risk it,* and after several rings a man answered at the other end of the line amid a crackling of static, and the man's voice, which she could not hear clearly, sounded abrupt, unfriendly, as if the ringing telephone had interrupted him at a time inconvenient to him, and she was saying in an unexpectedly anxious voice, *Matt? It's me—it's*—her voice breaking as she uttered her name. What pathos in so uttering her own name, her name uttered as a kind of plea, a kind of begging even as the man at the other end of the line said impatiently, *What? Who? Can't hear you,* for the line continued to bristle with static, like jeering laughter, as she repeated her name. How plaintive and piteous her voice, for she could not grasp the situation—was this man her lover? Had she caught her lover in a mood unlike any she'd ever known in him?—for in truth she barely knew him, their intimacy had been preceded by the briefest of acquaintances. Or had he sensed her ambivalence about calling him, at last on the morning of the third day of her absence, and was now taking revenge?—as rudely he said, *You've got the wrong number, sorry,* and hung up.

She was barefoot, shivering. In sweaty nightclothes and the most secret parts of her body throbbing with hurt, with insult and mute outrage, she found herself standing at the hotel window. With the most frantic bare hands you could not pry open such windows, nor could you smash them, for they were double- or triple-plated, unsmashable. *Ma'am you can't die, so easily. Throw yourself from a window?—no.*

She saw that it was 6:20 a.m. in Nevada—so early. In the east it was 9:20 a.m. and a reasonable time to have called him, she'd thought. Except he'd discovered something about her, in her absence. He'd discovered the elemental fact that he could live without her as she'd discovered that she could live without him. He was older than she by a number of years, he was more experienced and wiser, and why then should he need *her?* With his mouth he'd made love to her in a way that had unnerved and frightened her with its blunt intimacy, and now he was repelled by that intimacy and by her and wanted nothing more to do with her, *You've got the wrong number, sorry* in a voice thick with disgust, leaving her sickened, staggering. How swift and how deadly God's grace came as a spike in the heart. Telling herself with a measure of calmness, *This is my punishment. I knew better, I had been warned.* Yet like one stepping forward to the gallows, to allow the noose to be lowered over her head, perversely she saw herself take up the phone receiver again, there she was calling the number again, and after a half-ring the impatient man answered again as if knowing it must be her, whom he despised, and quickly in a pleading voice she said, *Matt this is Kathryn! Don't you know me—Kathryn?* And the reply was annoyed, grudging. *Look miss I'm not the man you want. I'm not "Matt." My last name is L—— but I'm not "Matt." I don't know who the hell you want but I'm not him—OK?*

The line went dead. The unknown L—— had vanished from her life as if he had never been.

This was a relief! Should have been a relief. But she was shaken, uncertain. Swaying on her feet as if she'd been struck on the head with a mallet—in such circumstances, the elemental fact is that one is still alive, still standing.

I will end this folly now. I can do this.

She seemed to be staring out a window—where?—a tall, wide plate-glass window she knew to be sealed, for her own protection: many and varied were the suicides of this famed city in the desert basin, but plunging from a high-rise window was no longer an option. The sun was now a fierce red-neon bulb beyond the mountains that were serrated like knife blades and flat-seeming like cardboard cutouts, and the city that had been glamorous and glittering by night was now flat, dull, and indistinct with the haze of air pollution, its mysteries exposed like cracks and stains in soiled wallpaper. She thought, *I have been warned. God has given me a second chance, to spare myself.*

She had not believed in God in a lifetime. Nor in any minimal secular god. She was contemptuous of such beliefs, but also envious. With no one to forbid suicide, you were more or less on your own.

Her room was on the twelfth floor in a hotel of approximately twenty floors. Not one of the newer hotels, nor one of the older glamorous hotels, rising totem-like amid the sprawl of the city—a safe neutral place she'd believed it, sufficiently distant from her point of origin and from her lover, whose face she'd begun to forget. His voice, she had forgotten: confused with the voices of strangers.

She'd decided not to call him, she'd been granted a second chance to spare herself, to avoid humiliation. And yet, with the blank open eyes of a sleepwalker she observed herself in the reflecting glass returning again to the phone—taking up again the lightweight plastic receiver with the heedlessness of one who, having been snake-bit, stung with venom, takes up again the glittery slumberous length of snake, coolly dry to the touch, both terrible and splendid, with a crazy smile. *Why not? Toss the dice.* Again, she dialed 411. Again, the appeal to *directory assistance.* But this time she requested *operator.* And with care she spoke to the operator—a woman with a just discernible southern accent. Kathryn spelled out her lover's name—so far as she knew it—and she spelled out the name of the suburban-rural road on which he lived; she explained to the operator that she'd been given two wrong numbers, in the past ten minutes, and this was a crucial matter, an emergency nearly, she could not afford to dial a wrong number again... In all this she remained polite, poised. You would not have guessed how close she was to screaming, cursing. Her reward was a third number, both like and unlike its predecessor.

Must have dialed this number, for suddenly—so very suddenly!—the phone was ringing—two thousand two hundred thirty-seven miles to the east—ringing and ringing and abruptly then the line went dead.

What was this!—her lover's phone line had gone dead. Utter deadness, blankness she was listening to, out of the lightweight plastic mechanism. With a sob she broke the connection.

In a bureau mirror was a woman's face flushed and smudged as if partially erased. Her mouth resembled a pike's mouth, thin-lipped, frozen into a grimace, hideous. Madness pinged in the woman's blood like tiny carbonated bubbles. She thought *I am shorn of all pride. I am desperate, broken. I am an addict. I can stop this.* Yet she continued: she did not stop: her icy fingers punched out the very number the operator had given her another time, and another time the phone rang, and rang. She saw her lover staring at the phone as it rang—his face came to her now, his eyes narrowed and turned from her—but he had no intention of answering the phone, he had no intention of speaking to her. He wanted nothing further to do with *her.* But this time the ringing ended with a *click!* and a recorded voice came on—*This is Matt. Sorry I can't come to the phone, please leave a message, thanks*—and at once she recognized his voice, of course this was her lover's voice, how could she have mistaken another's voice for *his!*

She was physically weak now, exhausted. She felt the impulse to quickly hang up the phone, that the man's feeling for her would be untested. She foresaw never calling him again. Now that she had done it, and now that she'd heard his voice and knew him, and felt a jolt of recognition deep in her body, that she knew him, and wanted him, and knew the bond between them, that distance could not dissolve, she had the power to end it, and nothing further would be risked between them. Her pride would remain intact, in time she would forget him...

Yet she left a message for him, in a voice not so faltering as previously; as if leaving a message for her lover was the most natural thing in the world; in a rush of feeling she said she missed him, she was sorry to have left so quickly without saying goodbye, she gave him the hotel number—*If you want to call.* She added *I love you.* Quickly then she hung up the phone.

She laughed wildly, both hands over her mouth. Like a child who has muttered an obscenity that can't be called back.

Only just 6:43 a.m. and she was spent, exhausted. It was something of a shock—a mild shock—seeing how quickly the sun had risen now, above the mountains. For once sunrise began, it could not be slowed, or impeded. Of course the sun was not "rising"—the earth was "turning on its axis" toward the sun. Kathryn knew this, for what it was worth to know such things; in her brain was an arsenal of such knowledge, loosely attached to facts, her education which had not come to her inexpensively mostly a snarl like yarn or shoelaces in a duffel bag. In any case, this "sunrise" was a spectacular sight. She was a reluctant pilgrim, she was one who *saw*. How the sky in the east was brilliant blinding flame-red riddled with clouds vaporous and fleeting as thoughts. How the sky was crisscrossed with mysterious funnel-like bands of cloud that widened and thinned in the wake of what might have been fighter planes, though the planes weren't visible from where Kathryn stood.

Love you! I never said that.

Smiling to think that he might believe her. The thin-lipped pike's mouth in a cruel smile. *Let him believe what he wants!*

With clumsy fingers she was fumbling to remove the sweaty nightgown, which fell in a puddle at her feet. She kicked it free of her ankles, repelled. It was disgusting to her, to smell so frankly of her body—a rank animal smell—a sexual smell—she must scrub herself clean. *For the wages of sin is death. Everlasting death is the wages of sin,* she wished to believe; she might clutch at such a belief as one clutches at a wall, for support as the floor tilts, shifts, collapses. *Wages of sin, I am in love with sin. My body sick with sin.* She would step into the shower and turn the water on hot, hot as she could bear it, scalding hot to cleanse herself; better yet, in a scalding, steaming tub she might scald the interior of her body, up inside her belly where the man had been. Shut the bathroom door and the shower-stall door and the sound of the shower would be deafening, she would hear no phone ringing, she would not be tempted to answer any phone. *No more! I am finished.* Yet—so strangely—as if to spite her, the phone on the bedside table began ringing. She had not heard this phone ring before—a high-pitched bat's-cry ring that seemed to her utterly astonishing, unanticipated. Yet calmly and matter-of-factly, as if nothing was wrong—of course, what could be wrong?—it was only a ringing phone—a ringing phone in her hotel room on the twelfth floor of the high-rise hotel surrounded by desert—she went to answer the phone.

Seeing her hand above the receiver, trembling in anticipation. How ridiculous she was, to be so frightened! So in dread of what was to come, calmly thinking *I don't want this. I don't need this.*

Her numbed fingers lifted the receiver as a sleepwalker might have done, heedless, yet attentive; her voice, which was faintly quavering yet, at a distance of so many miles, might have sounded warm, assured, murmured *Hello,* and there came at once a man's answering voice, close in her ear in the sudden catastrophic collapse of all distance, as if he were in this very room with her, saying *Kathryn? For Christ's sake is that you?* and simply she said *Yes. It is.*

The Spanish Steps: Keats Departing

He hated that he could no longer taste
the thick risotto, the paved rosetta rolls
soft on the inside, cool globes of fruit

plucked from ashy soil, the quivering
curd cheese and leafy Puglian greens.
All sustenance—even his Chianti's *terroir*—

mocked him. And so, after weeks
of this effrontery, he took his dinner tray
and pitched it out the window. Pigeons swarmed.

Urchins got the silver. His landlady
watched it disappear and prayed death
would do the same to him. It wasn't long.

Groaning, she carted off his furniture,
his mourners looking on, and lit a fire
at midnight at the bottom of the steps—

all those ripe eyes drinking in the glitter.

ALAN SHAPIRO
Park Bench

Behind the bench the Drive,
before the bench the River.
Behind the bench, white lights
approaching east and west
become red lights
receding west and east
while before the bench,
there are paved and unpaved
pathways and a grassy field,
the boathouse, and the playground, and the gardens
of a park named for a man that
no one now remembers
except in the forgetting that occurs
whenever the park's name is said.
Left of the bench there is a bridge
that spans the river
and beyond the bridge around a bend
floodlights from the giant Dry Goods
that replaced the bowling alley
that replaced the slaughterhouse
are dumping fire all night long
into the river; but here
where the bench is
the river is black, the river
is lava long past its cooling,
black as night
with only a few lights
from the upper story of the trapezoidal
five-star hotel across the water
glittering on the water
like tiny crystals in a black geode.

Haunt of courtship,
haunt of illicit tryst; of laughter
or muffled scream, what
even now years later
may be guttering elsewhere on the neural
fringes of a dream, all this
the bench is empty of,
between the mineral river that it faces
and the lights behind it speeding white
to red to white to red to white.

ALAN SHAPIRO
Stone Church

A space to rise in,

made from what falls,

from the very mass

it's cleared from,

cut, carved, chiseled,

fluted or curved

into a space

there is no end to

at night when

the stained glass

behind the altar

could be stone too,

obsidian, or basalt,

for all the light there is.

At night, high

over the tiny

galaxy of candles

guttering down

in dark chapels

all along the nave,

there's greater

gravity inside the

the grace that's risen

highest into rib

vaults and flying

buttresses, where

each stone is another

stone's resistance to

the heaven far

beneath it, that

with all its might

it yearns for, down

in the very soul

of earth where it's said

that stone is forever

falling into light

that burns as it rises,

cooling, into stone.

ALAN SHAPIRO
Bookstore

As if hallucinations made of words
could hallucinate themselves beyond the words,
out of the books, out of the newest
on display behind the window, and the ones
on tables in the gloom or ranged on shelves
in different sections; out
of the pages building to betrayal,
out of the spectral signatures
of doom of boredom of deceit,
after the stranger comes to town,
before the girl's disgrace, before
the shadowy flood or fire,
the bodiless mimicries escape
tonight the tangling plotlines
into the bodies of the couple
kissing outside the store,
into the ardor of the way they kiss,
he leaning against her leaning back
against the window, his hands flat
on the glass above her head,
hers on his hips to draw him
farther forward while her leg rubs
up the inside of his thigh
and down, and up again,
higher and still higher,
while the books behind them keep their own sweet time,
serene because the wraiths return,
inevitably, tomorrow or next week
or years away and a cooler hand
will take the book and open to a passion much

more desolate for being mutual
and new and never ending
till the page is turned.

E. V. SLATE
The Sailor

It was more than a year since the bombings, but the rates were still very good. The travel agent who handled his business trips had arranged it all in a matter of minutes, and Leo and his wife would step foot on the island less than seventy-two hours after the idea had first come to him.

Of course there would be reminders here and there, but that didn't mean the island had lost its allure. All they had to do was avoid Kuta beach, with its Australian bars and now the empty lots planted with cleansing banana trees. The private beaches of Nusa Dua were what they could afford, given the current economy, and it was what the agent had assumed they wanted without even asking.

As the plane touched down at Denpasar, Leo took his wife's hand, or rather covered it with his own sweaty paw, and winked at her. Here was one of those moments you were supposed to stop and feel grateful for almost as soon as they happened. Well he was glad if not sufficiently grateful. Wasn't it all his own doing?

This would be a well-deserved reward for his wife but also for him—for those long hours at the factory outside Beijing, his eyes aching from the fluorescent lights, those sometimes disastrous miscommunications with his interpreter, Bicky, and especially for those first months when he had struggled to get everything up and going. The new hires had avoided taking on responsibility at first, they weren't used to that, but slowly things had progressed, if only because he made sure of it. He had nursed the kids along and made sure everyone knew what was expected of him or her—that was key—and now, finally, he told himself he could manage to be away for a week, as long as he had his phone with him, just in case.

Evelyn had been dying to come here for years; he knew that. She had bought the Lonely Planet guidebook before they ever left Boston. The edition was probably outdated by now, but she had brought it with her anyway and flipped through the well-worn pages again on the flight, with pen in hand this time. She already knew which restaurants she wanted to try in Ubud, if they were still in business. We'll see, Leo said. Not we'll see if we end up there, but we'll see if they are still open when we do.

Recently they had lost their driver, then both of their club memberships: the company was cutting back all around just when Leo no longer had the energy to talk himself up. He understood hard times, that they were always there like an undercurrent tossing rocks and debris to the surface. The Tiger economies had proved to be little more than paper cutouts, and the stock market had taken its predictable, hysterical dive. His company shares weren't worth much of anything at the moment. He knew his bonus was next, maybe even a cut in base salary. The boss in Waltham had begun asking questions about Darwin, the local operations manager—How was his English, would he be able to handle calls from Europe and the States? Did he take ownership, was he (this said in a conspiratorial undertone) trustworthy?

He didn't confide in Evelyn. She had finally taken herself to the expat clinic and was trying a series of prescriptions for what she called her misfit moods. In the elevator each night, Leo would wonder what to expect when he opened the door. Two weeks before, he had come home to a silent flat. With no further evidence than that, he thought: she's done it. He opened the bedroom door, then the bathroom door. Finally he found her on the floor of their massive walk-in closet, clutching a pillow, sound asleep. She looked, as they always say of the dead, finally at peace. She had gone in there to think, she said later, to escape the droning of the AC, and then hadn't wanted to come out lest the maid see her in her pajamas. She said that when he woke her she hadn't known where she was or even who she was. For those few moments she had almost been happy.

The next day he called the travel agent, wondering why he hadn't made time for this sooner.

It was late, nearly ten o'clock at night by the time they claimed their luggage and wheeled through customs, nodding at the relaxed and smiling agents—"I guess we don't look like drug smugglers," Leo mused—and pulled up in front of a slender man in a wrinkled white shirt who was clutching a cardboard placard with their names scrawled in blue marker.

"Hynes the sauce?" the driver asked, pausing to light a cigarette. He had a rough, pockmarked face and shoulders too broad and heavy for his frame.

"That's the way you say it," Leo said, summoning an amiability he didn't feel—it wouldn't do to sock the first person they met on the island. "Though it's not the same family of course."

"Ah, like the Balinese, all named Wayan," the driver sneered.

"Wait, you're not from Bali?" Evelyn sounded alarmed.

He didn't look at her or offer to carry their bags, only said over his shoulder, as if muttering a curse: "Java."

They rode through the dark wet streets in silence. From the ID on the dashboard, Leo saw that the driver's name was Muhammad. Now there's an original name, he wanted to say. But this was not the time for joking, these were not the times. Nor the man. Muhammed was elementally grim, with a resentful glint in his eyes Leo had grown used to not seeing since leaving the States. Not only that, a fear was welling—something that he hadn't thought of before—that Evelyn might accuse him of bringing her here only after it had been bombed, the allure ruined and everything cheapened, as if this was all she deserved. He just wanted to get to the oasis of the hotel and start things off right. When they pulled off the main road and the sign of the hotel appeared, lit by a soft golden light in a thicket of foliage, Leo was relieved. He could tell Evelyn was too.

The Grand Puri Hotel had been modeled after a Hindu temple, with an entrance through a cleaved stupa and the reception area serving as the inner courtyard. The polished teak front desk was perhaps where the idols should have sat, in a real temple, but Leo and Evelyn did not have to pay homage there. Instead they were shown to a rattan couch, where the manager, wearing a fetching white headwrap, sat beside them to help them fill out the registration card. Bright orange papaya juices came on a platter and with the staff treating them so obsequiously, the gamelan music playing in the background so hypnotically, like chanting bells, Leo soon felt sleepy and placated—for what he didn't know or couldn't remember. It didn't matter. In the end very little does. But he didn't have the heart or the energy to complain about the rudeness of the driver.

Leo might have been aware that men of a certain age should not wear little red Speedos. Men with stomachs like a water buffalo's should really keep their T-shirts on at all times, even in the pool. But his protruding abdomen was hard, not hard like muscle, exactly, but hard like it had to be there. He was strangely fond of it and had a habit of pounding it absentmindedly with his fist, as he was doing now, walking past the deck chairs. He spread their towels and ordered drinks from the eager boy who appeared with the menu, and then he and Evelyn both lay back with the same sort of grunting exhale that, like old people, or people old before their time, they never heard themselves make.

"A day of rest," Leo said.

They had been busy, far too busy in Leo's opinion, as tourists for the last three days. They had visited temples on hillsides, temples by rice paddies, temples in the middle of town; they had tiptoed respectfully past the little offerings fashioned from folded banana leaves that appeared each morning along the sidewalks; they had been driven up to see the volcano and down to the various beaches, stopping at nearly every little artisan's shop along the way. They took in the bright green foliage, such a contrast to the gray dust and sickly trees of Beijing, and Evelyn even showed interest in learning the names of all the tropical flowers. They had eaten *nasi campur,* snake fruit, and every night a fresh *garoupa* that stared benignly at them from the plate. They grew used to the beauty of the locals and their gentle, beguiling ways. Even the touts seemed hurt if you were rude to them, and so Leo tried not to be the abrupt lout he had become in China. The black-and-white sarongs that the idols wore, symbolizing the balance of good and evil, Leo and Evelyn called "those ubiquitous tablecloths." And if they bickered or if she fell into one of her funks, which still washed over her in waves, they could always count on the soothing effects of the buffet dinner and shadow puppet show at the hotel to set things right enough for the next day.

If they worried about the local economy or the possibility of another attack, they didn't discuss it. After a minor accident on the road back from Lovina, a scraping of fenders when they tried to overtake on a hill, the two drivers settled it between themselves on the side of the road while Leo and Evelyn sat in the back seat as unconcerned as children.

The problem for Leo was that he didn't know, or he had forgotten, what they were doing here. As if going through a list, they had inspected the island according to the recommendations in the guidebook—but why? Yes, to see it and, yes, they had seen it. To give himself something to do he took hundreds of photos, none of them featuring Evelyn, who hated to have her picture taken, but now his memory card was full and he had no idea what he would do with the images, except keep them as some sort of proof. Maybe hang one or two in his office.

He watched his wife applying creamy sunblock. She had a trim figure for her age and boyish muscles in her arms, but her skin draped in two folds from her neck and crinkled, worn out, at her elbows and knees even though her weight had never varied much and she had never had the burden of carrying a child. She touched herself with gentle, fond concern—no brisk slapping as when Leo did this job for himself. Inside she must still think of herself as a woman of child-bearing age, with a desirable, even cherished body. He loved and pitied her for this. He had loved and pitied her for a long time, though somewhere along the way the ratio had changed.

There were times, especially in the beginning, when everyone expected him to "act his age," to set off on his own after graduation. But by that time he had no friend in the world but her, the American literature professor who had lost her job because of him, and she had waited for him in her old Toyota that reeked of cigarettes while he submitted his thesis to the department's secretary, who would not and had not met his eye since the scandal broke.

"We haven't burned at all, isn't that amazing?" she asked, applying a second coating to the tops of her hands.

"We've been careful. It makes you damn hot though, wearing that stuff, like a second skin. I'm going in to cool off." He hauled himself up and tugged at the elastic pinching his backside.

"Aren't you supposed to wait half an hour after eating?"

"That's nothing but an old wives' tale," he said without thinking.

"I've never had a stomach cramp in my life," he added. With that he dove into the deep end, displacing so much water that he doused Evelyn's toes and making such a splash that everyone around the pool looked up in momentary alarm.

It was a shallow dive, but immediately he started to sink and had to work vigorously to gain any speed at all. It had been a while and the first time in this middle-aged body, but he soon got the hang of maneuvering his bulk in the water. He did a lap, breathing on each stroke, left off the regulation turn, and then came back with a college-taught crawl, perfect in technique. He had taken lessons all four years on some sort of self-improvement program—ashamed of all the things he hadn't had the chance to learn in his factory town in Pennsylvania.

He stood up in the shallows, sunscreen running into his eyes, running off his stomach and making greasy rainbows on the surface of the pool. The sky was a deep, saturated blue without a cloud or puff of wind. The leaves of palms and coconut trees were stiff and shiny, as if made of plastic. His heart pounded in his chest like a motor that had just been given a kick-start. All right, all right, it seemed to exclaim. He had done all right, done the right thing. He had not been cruel.

For some reason he was reminded of an old movie they had seen long ago at the Brattle, on what became their first date. It was after they had read "The Swimmer" in class and Evelyn had invited the entire class to a showing of the film. He, like a sucker or more like a suck-up, had been the only one to go.

"Hey Eve," he called, drifting back near their chairs. He leaned over the edge of the pool and landed a good spit into the drain. "Remember, you know, way back when, 'The Swimmer'?"

She put down her magazine and regarded him through her fashionably large and round sunglasses. She had a small head and wispy short hairstyle that set off her fine features. Long before he knew her, she had been a pert, finely made girl—never a hippy or flower child, never a follower; pretty girls didn't have to be, though they so often were. But these sunglasses were ridiculous. They made her look like an alert, friendly insect, so unlike herself, and Leo tried not to smile whenever she turned to face him. This time he couldn't help himself.

"Yeah, remember how he swam home through the suburbs, from

pool to pool, meeting all his neighbors along the way? It would be something to do that here, swim along this strip, from resort to resort, and then back across this little bay. It would take all afternoon though."

She lifted her glasses, and squinted at him. Her mouth went sour, disappointed, as if she had been expecting him to say something else. "You're not really thinking about doing that."

"Come on, come with me," he said, though he hoped she wouldn't.

"Of all the things I could do right now, that's just about the last..." she said, adjusting the straps on her swimsuit, a black one-piece made hectic with white drawings of hibiscus. Leo knew that she didn't like to walk in front of people in it, would even keep a towel wrapped around her hips all the way to the edge of the pool.

"Well, I could use the exercise." He bobbed up and down in the water.

"And I don't think you're really allowed to swim in those other pools."

"I don't care." He waded over to the ladder and pulled himself out, struggling a little when the water seemed to want to pull him backwards. He stood dripping in front of her. "But if that's your attitude I'm not going to name the river after you."

"What's that supposed to mean?" She snatched up her magazine again and gave him an appraising look. "You're not going around like that, are you?"

He looked down at his hairy white expanse. He couldn't see his Speedo, could barely see the tips of his feet. "How else? Should I put on a business suit?"

The sand was hot, the sun fierce and punishing as soon as he broke away from the shade of the palm trees and the prickly lawn bordering the resort, and he had half a mind to turn back. But he couldn't do that—Evelyn wouldn't even have finished the page she was reading. When a man sets off and a woman sits weaving or whatever else she does to ravel time and make it shorter, he faces ridicule if he returns too soon. Leo would have to complete the journey and even name the damned river after her. Anyway, he didn't have all that far to go. He quickly came to and passed by the cushioned wooden lounge chairs of the next hotel, shaded by bright blue canopies, rather nicer than the shabby thatched ones at the Grand. He nodded at or gave a wincing smile—his feet really were burning—to the guests laid out in various states of slumber, like patients in need of deep rest and sun therapy. Bullion blond hair, glistening brown skin, round bottoms on display (like offerings), the sloping contours of stomachs: he had an urge to trail his hand, in appreciation, in worship even, from girl to girl. This is what he could have had all along! His heart, and the extension of his heart, swelled at the sight of them, lazy and sleeping in the sun.

Come with me, he wanted to say, as the swimmer had said to that young girl, the babysitter, he met along the way. Come with me, even though my wife, as far as I'm willing to admit, is waiting at home. In the movie, she had gone some way with him, if Leo remembered correctly, at least as far as the next estate and the next pool, but then had become disgusted by his advances; he repelled her, as Leo would repel these girls. Beauty, after all, seeks its own reflection, or the equivalent thereof. And he had lost his chance, not lost but renounced it.

He invaded the premises of the resort nearly dancing on his burned feet, and waded into the pool. What relief: the water was a little warm, like a child's bath, when he really could have used a cold withering dunk, but he was glad nevertheless. He executed a plowing sort of breaststroke with his head jutting above the water. The rooms here curved around the circular pool, with spacious balconies, each with a potted frangipani tree and tall sliding glass doors. There must be some rule about not hanging out one's towels or trunks. His room at the Grand looked over a small rather burnt lawn, and he certainly did put out his wet towels and Speedos, but in a place like this, on an island, one wanted to keep the sea and the water, even from the pool, in sight. Maybe he would move over here with Evelyn for their last few days; she would be surprised, and pleased, with an upgrade.

Back again to the hot beach, the sun sinking to an angle that sent the full brunt of the rays against the side of his cheek. He was parched, with no one handing him drinks left and right, like they had the swimmer. No one had handed Leo anything, not that he had ever felt resentful. All he really needed, he discovered, when the bills began piling up and Evelyn found herself blacklisted in a way a male colleague never would have been, was the boldness to stride right into the director's office, dodging the arrows of pink slips, and announce, "I'm the man for the China job, and let me tell you why."

It was all an act, of course, like something out of a William Dean Howells novel or Jimmy Stewart movie, but it had worked. Do your homework, offer yourself on the cheap at first, the years of your youth and vigor to open a factory across the globe. All on his own and without one bribe paid out that he knew about. He nearly jogged to the next hotel—a quiet, lush compound of white-canopied gazebos filled with orange and red cushions and densely overgrown thickets of bougainvillea and hibiscus—and quickly found the sleek poolside bar.

"Give me a glass of water," he said thickly, wiping the sweat from his forehead.

"Yes sir," the bartender said. "Gas or no gas?"

"No, not from a bottle. Just a glass of water. Free. I didn't bring my wallet, see." He indicated his healthy stinking nakedness.

"Just charge to your room," the waiter suggested.

"I, ah, don't want to do that. Just give me a goddamned glass of water."

The waiter poured from a small Evian bottle. "No charge," he said.

"Oh, all right. No tap water here?" He drank it in one tilt and then regarded the empty glass. "And, yeah, sorry about that."

"No problem, sir."

"I guess you're used to, you know…"

"Arseholes like you?" An older man, thin and drawn, with a shock of fine white hair that had surely once been blond, and so deeply tanned that here and there, on his nose and forearms, he seemed charred, smiled at him from the other end of the bar and raised his glass. Two straight furrows etched into his cheeks stretched sideways with this smile and gave him a roguish look. "I suppose he is, since I come here all the time. Kadek, refill this and one for our friend as well."

A real drink then: whiskey, just what a man on an adventure needs, and then another, all on George's tab, though Leo really would have preferred a Foster's or even lemonade: something more hydrating.

"Thanks, and, ah, come over to the Grand later and let me return your hospitality," Leo said. He had told George about his journey and also about the movie, the tragedy at the end when the swimmer finds an empty house, no longer his, his wife and children gone. However, the story seemed to lose pathos as he retold it and he grew somewhat flustered. Maybe the tragedy would have been if he had returned home and nothing at all had changed, he suggested with sarcasm in his voice that he didn't feel. He swayed on his stool and had to grab the bar. No, George had answered with a steady gaze. "I'm afraid I don't see the tragedy there unless the poor sod didn't realize what he had when he had it. That's every man's tragedy though; it's certainly been mine."

He finished his drink and swirled the ice in the glass as if looking for his fortune in the arrangement of the melting cubes. "I would take you up on that, but I'm setting off tomorrow," he said, pointing out the furled sail of his white sloop, just visible through the slim bars of the coconut trees. "Back to Denpasar, sell the boat, and then back to merry old England. I've had enough, I daresay, more than enough of this."

"Enough of paradise, of adventure?" Leo asked, incredulous.

George had been sailing around Southeast Asia for two years and had even encountered pirates on a motor boat off the shores of Malacca. They gave chase, fired a couple of rounds; he answered with one report of his shotgun, the recoil of which nearly sent him backwards off the deck. "Gave me a shock. Must have them too. We both seemed to say the hell with it, and went our own ways." He shrugged tiredly when Leo pressed him for more of the story, refusing to offer any embellishments.

Now he smiled sadly at the word *paradise*. "You might say that. I'm going home to help my son and daughter-in-law. They just bought a cottage in Dorset that is in need of repair, and then I've never even seen the new grandbaby, Elisabeth." He fished into the back pocket of his shorts and pulled out his wallet. Oh no, Leo thought, here it comes. Those snaps they take at the hospital: the baby's face swollen, misshapen, grimacing—not at all resigned to being born. But George only pulled out some crumpled rupiah and paid the tab.

"Enjoy your jaunt, old boy," he said, knocking Leo softly on the shoulder. "But don't stray too far off the path, if you know what I mean. It's a bitch trying to find it again and then you might wish that you had never left home in the first place. Those who said the earth was flat and we shouldn't go near the edge might have been onto something."

Yes, he would—enjoy himself, that is. He stumbled across the lawn and then righted himself. He would enjoy himself very much, thank you for asking, because unlike poor George he was still in the thick of it, still in the game; feel that—his biceps, his triceps: tough gristle hiding under some insulation, that was all. Yes, underneath he felt as young as when he had first met Evelyn.

The sun had slipped behind the rounded hills, and the sky over the sea had gone pink and seemed unaccountably empty with neither clouds nor a moon, though the water itself was dark and would be black by the time Leo swam home, the tide full of jellyfish. But Leo didn't mind. He was revved up, fully charged, and on a mission of his own bidding. He would swim the last resort, already illuminated by golden lamps and Christmas lights at the end of the beach, and then make it back in time to meet Evelyn for a victory dinner.

By the time he marched onto the manicured grounds, through the trees wound with lights, and past the poolside lounge chairs, abandoned now with towels left here and there like discarded bandages, the outdoor restaurant had been set for dinner. Candles flickered and the cutlery shone. Three-tiered, red-tasseled umbrellas sheltered each table. A hidden band was playing a soft, watery melody. The early diners, some older couples and a few young families with children, all looking tanned and rested, their hair still wet from their showers, watched Leo as he tramped past them in his red Speedo. A waiter followed him for a few steps and then turned back to consult with the manager.

Leo dove into the infinity pool (a bit of a belly flop, but no matter) and got on with his crawl, kicking up foam behind him. The water was satisfyingly cool. This time, since it was deep enough, he did the regulation turn. He knew he was being watched, and so he did two laps of breaststroke and then a ridiculous, thrashing attempt at a butterfly, which brought him back where he began, gagging, his chest aching. He had drunk water, salty with sweat, and his throat burned from the chlorine. He hauled himself out of the deep end with his last ounce of strength, nearly landing flat on his stomach, and tottered away, his feet slipping on the tiles and bats the size of small rocks skimming past his head.

Utterly lost. I am. That's what he thought: those words, that sequence. He was wandering between bungalows, trees and bushes, passing by gates that gave glimpses of small circular pools and Jacuzzis and narrow private paths. Unobtrusive signs indicated the names of these hidden locations, Lotus Villa and Nutmeg Chalet, but not the way back to the beach or even to the main pool. In the daytime this would all be clear, he thought.

Then he was creeping through some prickly shrubbery, hoping that he would not be discovered. He had to find his own way out of this mess. Where were the bats now? Mosquitoes were feasting on his broad sweating back. He was hungry and sickeningly drunk. He stumbled up an incline of sand, thinking this must be it: the beach, finally, and when he came down on the other side, all he could say was, Oh shit.

They were sitting around a fire, as men had sat around fires on these islands for thousands of years. They looked at Leo and the orange light flickered over their ancient features. Muhammed stood up slowly and narrowed his eyes with hatred. Leo stumbled toward him and then stopped. I made a wrong turn somewhere, he said, and his voice sounded tinny and far away. Muhammad, off-duty, was dressed in a torn t-shirt and baggy cotton shorts. He muttered something to the others and then spit over his shoulder. An older man, smoking a thin pipe and bobbing his crossed leg, argued with him, making chopping motions with his hands. Then he, too, got up, and he and Muhammed seemed to thrust their chests at each other. Muhammed ducked his head, backed down. He came toward Leo, his flip-flops pounding into the sand, an awful sound. Leo backed away, but he was pulled quickly by the arm and pushed onward toward the trees. A couple of the other men jumped up and followed them.

Other tourists had come to ends like this, sent on long marches single file through the jungle, only to end up shot or hacked to death. Those doe-eyed missionaries in the Philippines, those hapless trekkers in Uganda. He remembered reading the stories in the newspapers and thinking: The fools! Paying good money to go off to volatile places where they didn't belong, practically offering themselves up as victims.

He stumbled over roots that stuck out of the ground. Branches lashed his face. He wanted to put a stop to this, he wanted to be a man, but he was barefoot and panting, and when he didn't move fast enough, Muhammed nudged him from behind.

Under the trees, there was no light. Even the animals seemed afraid, and who is to say they weren't? They squawked and squealed as Leo flailed through shrubs with urine burning down his leg. Muhammed finally shoved him, hard, and Leo fell out onto wet grass. The sprinklers were on. His hotel towered above him with its tepid yellow lights and the sounds of women's laughter and the soft dong-dong-dong of the gamelan.

People had gathered in the lobby of the Grand waiting for the dining room to open, clutching orange and yellow drinks choked with slices of fruit. Leo had been wandering, lost, in identical hallways. He had found a fire escape map on a wall and he knew he had to cross this open space to get to his room. He hunched in his shoulders and kept his hands cupped in front of his crotch. The marble floor was cold under his feet. Walk quickly but not so quickly that you call attention to yourself. Duck your head. Lower. He heard the laughter, but didn't look up. He made it to the elevator, and rode up shivering.

Knock on your own door. Knock louder. And then it opened, as doors had opened for him his entire life, but only because he kept knocking and then pounding—never because, except for his affair with Evelyn, he had picked the lock.

FAITH SHEARIN
Being Called Ma'am

The summer I turn forty I pretend I am still young enough
to sit with my college self at the library before disappearing

in a field of smoke. Don't my jeans still fit? Can't I see
without glasses if I just hold the book a little farther

from my face? Then, hiking with my daughter, I find
myself talking to a group of college boys, the sort

I would have gone camping with twenty years before,
their faces like unused maps. And when they answer

they call me ma'am, that word their mothers taught them,
or some old schoolmarm maybe, demanding respect.

A distance opens between the woman they see and the one
of my imagination and I am not someone they might laugh with

in the library but instead the stern face that appears from
behind the stacks to remind them of their manners.

I am the finger over the lips: sexless, as heavy as silence.

FAITH SHEARIN
Not Knowing

It is the not knowing that keeps us going,
the way we turn the pages of a book.

We don't know which October will bring
hurricanes and which will bring

the bright Conchs that hold open
our doors. We don't know whether

the Blue Heron is pensive
on his big stick legs or if he

has seen a fish. We don't know
whether the sea turtle's eggs will hatch

and, if they do, how many will find
the tide's tongue. We don't know if

the sick dog will get better, if
the argument continues or resolves.

We don't know which year the whales
will pass so close we could touch

their slick backs with our hands.
We try not to know that the story

is short: what matters now will vanish
like snow. We wonder if a friend

will visit, if a gift will arrive, if our children
will come home dusted in happiness.

Our island is disappearing: each year
another row of cottages erased by wind.

Still, we wonder which bright box will hold
on to the sand, which castle will last until noon.

FAITH SHEARIN
The Old Boyfriends

They return in my father's ghostly sailboat,
never steady, and in spring when my body

is like a maple tree. Their purpose is to imagine
the life we did not choose. One lives in a house

with a cat, mountains in the distance. Their job
is to tend my younger self: that other body.

One is hiking by day, carving cabinets at night.
They are just as I left them or they left me.

They are in my daughter's questions,
in the towns where I was young. I left one

in a restaurant after the food was ordered
so he dined alone with two burritos, two iced teas.

CHARLIE SMITH
It Gets a Little Hazy About Now

The years in Cuba are behind me now.
Little spotted dogs, like tiny archangels
followed me around. I smelled of salt
and palm oil. Given the nature

of belief, the effectiveness of the divine will,
unforgettable and strictly
for the birds, I could be said
to be out of touch. I read Aeschylus—

the diaries—*Othello on the Beach*,
and Peter Gunn. I gave my change
to private charities, something personal
I devised. Her lipstick

smelled like a clown's face. We practiced
tricks the Ringling brothers taught her.
I supported small retainers,
converts and muralists struggling with

the dialect. We waked,
often at dawn, and lay
in the sheets cursing quietly. *I will
particularize and dissuade*, she said,

but it made no difference. I wore hats
of coconut frond and drove a Russian car.
My retreat from life
fit like a glove. Some nights

strange memories, passing for dreams,
of mud-caked shoes, cats
on the table eating scraps, and young men
caressing the faces of their superannuated lovers.

I shivered sometimes. I was on a long run
of quirky asides. *Take the monkey*, she said, *and go.*

JEFFREY THOMSON

Where Do Your Poems Come From?

For Karen and Aria

> *In the Namib fat sand rats saunter through*
> *all the continents of their own personal deserts*

I started this poem thinking about Orpheus,
because I am always thinking about
Orpheus, strumming as the dead stir

> *all the while, looking for death's hawk-shaped smear,*
> *looking for amaranth seeds small as the ball bearings*

in the black thickets of Hades, the weeping
King and only the Queen dry-eyed.
This poem began for me as I thought

> *of the plane that taxis off the dirt track*
> *runway and yanks itself into the sky*

of my grandfather waking me to go fishing
in the early dark, even though
he never speaks to me as he opens

> *meter by meter, the uneven slosh of the petrol*
> *in the wing tanks and sway of the plane in the wind*

the door of this stanza and stands
in a sharp wedge of light. When
I was growing up, a friend and I traveled

> *as the pilot follows the spikes and hoops*
> *of vertebrae speckling the dunes come from*

miles to sneak into an abandoned sand factory,
the catwalks and vats, the webbing of the windows
in the late light. So now when I begin

>*the bray of the surf as it punts into the shore,*
>*kicked there by a wind that began in*

this poem talking about the lonely
architecture of memory, you know that
that is what I mean. I spent an afternoon in

>*Pôrto Seguro as the six-hour breath of the Amazon*
>*huffed into the sea and the bore tides rode*

Riomaggiore and watched cats come down
from the crumble of houses chasing each other
into the Gulf of Genoa. They came down

>*their stampede back into the trees, into the dim dim*
>*forever dim twilight of the forest in the Tahuayo*

as the fishing boats returned late in the day,
gathered around the beached hulls, and
waited for the heads and spare bait, waited

>*where hyacinth macaws gnaw at hillsides*
>*of clay and nest in the great almonds*

for the gift of a glassy eye. Late that night,
returning quite drunk from a café up
the coast, our boat pulled into the city

>*in a ruckus as a blessing of rain muscles*
>*through the trees in the heat of the day, and*

with only a few lights speckled up the sides
of the dark hills. The bakers were at work
and the town smelled of bread and yeast and

    in the sudden silence full of ticking
    as the rain finishes, and from the cane chair

warmth rising to the thin spackle of stars—
that's where this poem comes from—we bought
hot bread and tore into it in the dark

    beneath the awning where I write in a book
    blanked by the last angle of the setting sun.

... a message. The only Marty I ever knew. Maybe he said his last name, but he didn't need to. Forty years, so what? I was back there in a high school desk. Do they still have them, that funny s-shaped chair with the storage box below, a 2 x 2 or less to write on, tilted toward your stomach so the pens roll down if you miss the slot?

I listened to the message and saw his rounded shoulders, his waving hands—pen in one, always, or pencil, maybe. Saw his jerky motions as he gestured back at me or across to me or poked my shoulder. I can't remember what the classes were or what we learned, but I know his whisper (never much whisper in it), the angled softness of his hair and shape and voice.

Then I was back scrubbing my refrigerator shelves, and what I thought was I won't call him back. Too much trouble, too much chaos in his life, I'd heard. Too much for my measured space.

I didn't have a choice. I knew that, even as I reasoned with who I was now.

I didn't cry then, when he first called. I wasn't much of a crier.

By the time I answered him, I'd been talking to him in my head most of the night and part of the day.

"Marty," I said. "Julie."

"I didn't think you'd call," he said.

That was all and I was back there; I could see his fingers threading the pen over under, under over.

"Forty-one years," he said. "How are you?"

I laughed. "You and your numbers. Well, you know, I've got a chemistry quiz—I could use some help." I wanted to say, "I'm still pretty. I look the same."

We talked awhile. Mostly he did, I think. I asked questions, looked for the outline of his decades, looked for something—I couldn't say what. I glossed over my husbands, long gone, my very visible career, the easy *comfort of how I lived now—gently crafted his view of me, tidied up the corners of the months and years.*

He lived in Denver. He had a law degree he'd never used except to get his daughters back in school when they got kicked out. He read and reread The Brothers K.

"I didn't think you were captive in our Russian phase," I said. "Kip, Louise, certainly Stevie, we read them all senior year."

"I can't remember," he said. "I connect Dostoevsky with all of us, but I can't remember which books I read when." Actually what he said was "I connect Dostoevsky with all of you."

The second time he called, we mostly talked of who we had been. The weeks between the calls, the person I'd become disappeared and I was 16, 17, fey and gangly and full of budding anarchy and hope. Not jaundiced and habitual and knowing.

The conversation begun, we continued back and forth. It lasted like this a year or two.

And then, one morning, with another phone call, it was over, he was done, and I was left knowing he had dared me and I'd failed. Me, the one he coached through chemistry and math, he was teaching me still in his smart, erratic way. He was teaching me what I didn't want to learn. Didn't then, didn't now. Couldn't, maybe.

That's when I cried and kept on crying.

I should say, the next day, the day after the last call, my mother died. It was that kind of year all year. I couldn't get up from my knees before a stray but well-placed punch nailed me down again. Marty started it. But then he always had.

We were odd kids, the two of us. Our friends as well. Perhaps, we were crippled to begin with.

I met Marty in seventh grade—I remember it as the year I learned too much and nothing. We had a teacher, Mrs. Patton, she wasn't smart, couldn't teach. One of us, maybe Marty, mimicked her pronunciation of pumice, waggled his chin like she would do with her turkey gobbler neck. "Pummy," he said and shook a little and we laughed and were rude together.

So it went, she tried to teach and we muzzled grins behind our hands. It got worse, of course it did. Mrs. Patton looked more and more befuddled as we escalated into dropped school books and flapping elbows.

"*Remember Patton?*" Marty said.

"*Pummy. That was daylight for me. I never knew it was possible, to mock an adult.*"

"*Not me, it was habit.*"

"*You were ahead of me even then. I was always perfect for adults.*"

I heard a sniff of laughter and saw the half smile of his mouth through the miles of air.

"My parents, you know," I said. "*Dinner at 5:30 sharp, elbows off the table. Our big idea of fun was Parcheesi night and popcorn with Mom and Dad. Paper party napkins folded just so.*"

"*Humph,*" he said, "*a board game with the Judge. Not likely. Maybe chess, but then it'd be a lesson.*"

By tenth grade, we were like siblings; we thought we knew each other so well. Not just Marty and me, but all thirty of us in our separate classes for smart kids. We made our own world, tried to learn who we were by trying roles that played well to the back row of AP English. There was an inner circle, a clique that paced the class—Kip, Louise, Stevie, Ellen, and me, Julie. Sheila was on the edges, muscling in and out. Marty was sometimes there, sometimes not; he was the disparate one in a litter of raucous thrivers. He was who he was, with or without us.

Marty was more mass, more eruptive, more everything really. He exploded—with contempt, or passion or disinterest or just movement. His notebook edges were covered in hard broad lines; geometric shapes pressed in on messy handwritten lists of Latin roots or American history dates. In all the classes we had together he fidgeted without a break. He was a smoker early and I don't think he quit. Although he was usually with me or Sheila, we knew he wasn't really there—he seemed peripheral in his own vision.

"Sheila lives somewhere near you," I said. "You should call her."

He answered with a snort before I heard him inhale.

"What? I always thought you had a thing for her?"

"Sheila?" he said.

"We were best friends the summer before ninth grade. She taught me how to make out, practice loving, we called it."

"Sheila?"

"No, not that. She gave me the chance—I watched her and whoever she was with. You know, in her basement. We were hanging out with boys that were friends."

"She taught me a few tricks too," Marty said. "But she was scary even then. I think I used her as cover—to take the attention off me in class."

"Remember when she whacked Kip in English? And scarred Pat in Earth Science with the pencil jab," I added.

"Yeah, but he trashed her science fair entry."

"Just bent it a little. I knew you liked her. I quit being friends with her around then, too unpredictable, too loud, you know. Ellen and I did volcanoes for Earth Science—ours didn't erupt."

I thought he had a crush on her.

We were happy together. We felt at home. I shouldn't say we. I was. I was happy. And Marty made it so (as did the others). His whispers and taps and abrupt gestures played some part in my audience, in the secret of my self-opinion.

"That was the day in Mrs. Wrigley's class. Sheila started it when she slapped Kip."

"I forgot that," I said. "Forgot Sheila came first. God, Wrigley was mad. We were such brats."

"She was a bad teacher."

I saw him on the other end of the phone, soft, thick hair flopped over his forehead. Stocky body that tended to soft as well. Moving parts is how he always looked though—fingers tapping, arms stretching, legs out and in with jiggling feet. Face, always amused, bemused, listening, angry, never quiet, never peaceful or silly or easy. I straightened the fringe of the rug with my toe as I gripped the phone.

"Sheila slugged Kip. Or rather she screamed and slugged him. He looked shocked and yelled something theatrical, like 'Oh God, I'm hit.'"

"I'm sure he did something nasty to her first," I said. "He pinched her, I think. There was a reason."

"And Wrigley said, 'that's it, we'll have an essay test.'"

"You were sitting behind me," I said.

"Yeah, forty-one years and I still remember it," Marty said. "It was a free for all. I thought Wrigley would croak when the back rows chimed in banging their books. A prison riot, that's how it sounded in the hall, the principal said. Damn. Lab partners in Chemistry. I never thought I'd pull you through."

"I knew you would. But I gave up for Physics. Mostly to give you a break. I bet Michigan was a breeze after that, without me to prep for math and science."

"It wasn't the same, wasn't the same at all."

"So tell me," I said. "Tell me about the years." I lay back down, fluffed the pillows straight. I heard a match strike on his end.

"Forty-one. Oh, you know, I've been around like everybody. Got married, had some kids, got divorced."

"Yeah, me too, except for the kids."

"Then my ex-wife got cancer and I took them all back in. She died and now the girls are close to gone, one out, one almost."

"Good God. How awful," I said. "How awful," I said again.

"Not really, not at all. The girls are great. I loved getting them back. And I always liked my ex. Sad. It was sad, but never awful."

Electricity. That's the word I want to describe us all together. We were either dreamy or electrified. Mostly by each other. After I learned to kiss, I couldn't speak in class for a year. I felt lit up bright orange; speech was too much, on top of the obvious fire of my skin. Marty's fidget was in my body, capped off.

"So call Sheila," I said. "She's divorced now, has a kid, I think."

"I have always loved you," Marty said.

"I never knew. I thought you had a thing for Sheila."

I thought I was his friend.

The summer of the driving licenses we all started to edge away from the mass of us. Before that we were always in a pack. Marty saw it all, he watched me. I think he knew Kip and I practiced kissing in the front seat of his dad's Chevy.

"Remember Crockett?" Marty said.

"Whew," I said. "How did they let us study Communism for a year?"

I hadn't thought about that hour in Crockett's class until now. Somewhere, somehow, I knew what happened to Marty that day could happen *to any of us if we let it show—the electricity under our skins, the passion tied in a package and shelved somewhere. Could have then, I felt, and now too.*

"She's dead, you know. Crockett. Heart attack, I think. Last year. Royce is the only one alive we liked. I loved the book reports."

"Even that, though, even that day in the principal's office, I felt safe. It was OK. I got off easy."

"Gotta go," I said. "Someone at the door." *I stared down at a woman at the bus stop and wiped a smudge from the windowpane.*

What had happened in Crockett's class that was so unspeakable? I went and rummaged for the last yearbook—our graduation year.

In one picture, Marty stands in biology lab with Kip and a couple of the more earnest, ass-kissing girls. He looks bemused, a normal Marty-look. Kip looks affected. Where was I? Probably back behind them on my lab stool next to Ellen, chattering on about the stupidity of science projects. I'm sure she promised herself she would never, ever partner with me on any project again. She hated all those projects we did together, I think now—from Krakatoa to The Great Awakening. I made up posters and words while she did the research; I presented while she supported. Not a problem, I can do it by myself, I would have said, if any of this had been spoken, which, of course, it never was.

Except if you were Marty.

I flipped the pages past the portrait shots where we all look young and washed. The Monopoly Club picture. We're all there. Almost all. We thought we would be ironic and smart or insular and odd, above it all. Our group, our inner circle, started a Monopoly Club the year we all took Communism. It was probably my idea. We had our picture in the yearbook's Career Club section. I wrote the copy myself. There's Ellen in the middle running the game on the grass behind the high school; everybody looks at her except me and Marty. That was Ellen's job of choice—boss man, the center, the smart, capable one. We rarely let her have it. There are a few other filler kids in the picture, thrilled to be included. Marty and I frame the shot, on either side. I'm standing, looking out into the future—tall and thin, bored but highly visible. He's on the opposite side, seated with his hand thrust out (fidgeting, no doubt) reaching, stretching, and looking to the center, but not at Ellen.

Absences are equally expressive—no Louise, no Kip. She would have found it silly and not worth her time, yet one more juvenile prank of mine. Kip had left us senior year in a snit with me for dumping him; or we might have excluded him, in retaliation for his departure.

It's an eerie look at who we were in the last moment and who we would become. No sign that we knew that our lives were set.

"I read a lot, The Brothers K, start it when I finish it. Sometimes Crime and Punishment."

"Too dark, too psychological. I couldn't read them now. I loop read Dickens, Dreiser, Trollope, Balzac. I like the panorama, the interlaced view," I said. "I write essays about it, you know, about economic cycles and fiction."

"I drove a cab awhile; the patterns are cool, quickest route, you know."

"And your girls?"

"They're like me. Hyper, quirky. Trouble, both of them. I love watching them—talking to them, being with them. They're great."

How can you live, how do you live? I wanted to say from my window seat far above the Avenue.

"God, Crockett was great. She worked like hell to make us use our minds. I was always extra-hyped in Crockett's class," Marty said.

Marty and I followed Louise down the stairs from Chemistry to Communism. He sat in front of me in this one, I hunched behind him. It was real; Crockett was smart and sharp, sarcastic sometimes. She was our God. It was a narrow room and our desks made a fan around her desk.

Crockett took her pulpit, front and center, notes on the podium. She was dressed like a person, not like the other teachers; she wore high heels and on her big frame, well-made dresses, earrings—gold buttons or heavy loops. We took notes, read the assigned extra essays for Crockett—no textbook for where she took us.

"Russian Revolution," she said. "Let's start with Hegel, Kropotkin, Bakunin. Marty, dialectical materialism, take us through Hegel."

I relaxed. I knew he knew. He was weaving his pencil in his right hand through his fingers as he talked. Thesis, antithesis, synthesis. A new order arises from the direct opposition to the existing situation.

The state moves through conflict, philosophical as well as possibly physical.

I ducked down lower and passed a note to Kip, ride home? it said. He lived near me.

Whack, Marty's hand hit the desk. "Damn it, you've missed the point," he yelled.

I didn't know what happened. Miss Crockett was moving toward us, her face tight and red.

"Out," she said. "Front office. That, Mr. Schmidt, was unacceptable."

And he was stacking notebooks, up and out the door before I could do more than sit up and look around.

"Jim," Crockett said. "Take us up to Marx." Jim was good for words, loved the sound of eddies of sharp political phrases; he'd talk until the bell rang while Crockett policed the rows for further revolution.

We were in the car after school. It was Kip and Ellen and me.

"What happened?" I said.

"He diverted to the psychological impact of dialectical materialism and the turmoil mirrored in a person. He'd started on the personality of Marx and what it must have cost him. He was waving his arms and stabbing the air with his pencil and talking louder and louder. She interrupted to get him back on track and he blew," Ellen said.

"Oh, Lord," I said. "Marty. I should have paid attention. I could have stopped him. I know I could have."

"Conduct, probably," Ellen said. "Who cares about that? Just an unacceptable display, really. He didn't mean it."

"An eruption, a pimple," Kip said, "a visible one. But God she was mad. I've never seen her lose it."

"His father will kill him," I said. "We can think anything we want, but act like that in Crocket's class?"

"I made good money gambling until the casinos blacklisted me," he said. "That paid the mortgage."

"Numbers," I said. "Of course."

"I couldn't really hold a job for long. I'd explode and hit the road."

I shook my head, sunk my teeth into my top lip.

"The girls are almost gone now, the youngest out this summer prob-

ably. They're great. I wish they had what we had. All that freedom, all those books. Crockett. She didn't even frown at me the next day, went on like we always did."

Even now, he brought back the memory of what we were and weren't. *We were always in our heads. To connect heart and intellect was a scandal—the jumble of emotion guttering from our bodies found channel in metered essays and sarcastic turn of phrase. Except for Marty.*

The rain stopped. The sky lightened in the picture window behind the baby grand. Marty finished the sonata he played in an almost ironic way and looked up, we all did.

"The Park," I said.

"The Park," Kip said.

We were all out the door, racing down the hill of Stevie's driveway, strung out on the narrow road past the quarry, then balancing across the log to the swings. I made it first, of course. I pumped higher, flung my hair back, the chino four-gored skirt flapping up. They watched me, Kip and Marty and Ellen, even as Stevie took a swing and eddied back and forth and back with Louise behind him giving him a push now and then. Then Kip and Ellen joined us and only Marty remained, leaning against a tree watching the rest of us ebb.

Afterwards we walked back up to Stevie's and watched Marty continue up the street to his house. Ellen and Kip and I—she was driving that day—went off together.

"I have always loved you," he said.

"I didn't know," I answered. But I did, I did.

I was dying to get to college. I wanted away from the smallness of our set. I wanted to be invisible and new-made. But that fall when I left, the longing started. I missed it, all of it, not just the talk.

It was never quite the same. Marty and I rode around in his father's car all the next summer, when I wasn't working. He'd wait at the counter for me to get done waitressing. We listened to music endlessly— "Hey Jude" over and over. I can't remember what we talked about.

After that we all drifted apart for decades until the year before Marty's call.

"Julie?"

"Speaking," I said and listened hard to place the voice I knew.

"Kip."

"Kip," I said. "Kip." I sat down at my desk chair, stared at a screen of some garbled words of book review I had labored on, would again, no doubt, if my world reformed.

I broke the silence. "I know," I said. "I guess I know."

It was February. The winter wind shook the windows of my world.

"He went out in the snow in his front yard in Denver and shot himself."

"No." I said. "Why not a pill? Why not a creeping, peaceful sleep?"

"Marty?" he said.

"Damn it," I said. "Damn him," and I hung up the phone.

I leaned into the rattling sill and lifted the frame as high as it would go and reached my torso into the fifteen stories down before I pulled back.

Who will love me now? Who will love me now? I slammed the window shut and turned my back.

The next day my sister called about my mother and made me lean, again, far out and yell this time, "Who? Who will love me now?"

It's been like that ever since.

ABOUT ELIZABETH STROUT
A Profile by Ladette Randolph

In a *Washington Post* article, Elizabeth Strout discusses how, as a girl, she played people-watching games with her mother. Together, they would imagine the lives of strangers they saw around town. "It seemed to me," Strout says, "from an early age, that nothing was ever as fun as that…The first ambition I remember having was that of becoming a writer. It seemed as natural as the fact that I would have another birthday…it did not seem a wish, but a fact of life."

Strout, the author of the bestselling novels *Amy and Isabelle* and *Abide with Me,* and a collection of linked stories, *Olive Kitteridge,* goes on to describe how her mother gave her notebooks and told her to write down what she had observed that day. "The idea was not to tell a story," Strout writes, "but to record the experience of the man selling me sneakers…so that recording the world was part of my first clear memories."

Despite her early ambitions, Strout had a circuitous route to authorship. She published her first short story, "The Suicide's Daughter," in *New Letters* after she graduated from law school at Syracuse. "I showed it to a few people," Strout recalls. "No one said anything." And it took another few years before she published a second story. In those early years, she was so reticent about her work that few people even knew she was a writer.

During that time, however, she had also started writing the novel that would eventually become *Amy and Isabelle.* The ten years she invested in that novel paid off, for it was instantly recognized by critics as a major achievement and went on to become a made-for-TV movie produced by Oprah Winfrey.

Amy and Isabelle dealt with the dark, unspoken rivalries in mother/ daughter relationships, and the secrets inherent in the lives of seemingly everyday people in small towns. Described in a *Newsweek* review as "a kind of modern *Rapunzel,*" the novel touched a chord with many people, not only for its subject matter but for the beauty of its sentences.

Another eight years passed before she published her second novel, *Abide with Me*, a distinct departure from *Amy and Isabelle*. The story of a young minister in a small town in 1950s Maine, struggling with his faith in the wake of his wife's premature death, it too met with acclaim. As a *New Yorker* review says, "Strout has created an absorbing world peopled by characters who argue the merits of canned cranberry sauce…meanwhile dark fears…run beneath the surface of their lives like water under ice."

Three years later, she published *Olive Kitteridge*, which netted her the 2009 Pulitzer Prize and brought her work to the attention of an even wider audience. The collection's title character, Olive Kitteridge, who Louisa Thomas in *The New York Times Book Review* describes as being "like a planetary body, exerting a strong gravitational pull," is a large, awkward, opinionated New England woman who succeeds in winning readers' hearts, even as she sometimes shocks them with her unblinking honesty. As Thomas goes on to say, "she isn't a nice person," but she regularly surprises the reader with her "remarkable…empathy." Even if some readers don't like Olive, no one can forget her, and she seems destined to enter the canon of permanent American literary characters.

What all of Strout's work to this point has in common is small New England towns. Having descended from many generations of New Englanders, Strout's knowledge of the region is bone deep. Her father, a parasitologist, was on the faculty of the University of New Hampshire's Animal Sciences department, specializing in tropical parasites (an irony not lost on Strout), and the family lived in New Hampshire during the week, but Maine remained their emotional home throughout her childhood.

Although she does not speak directly of her father's influence on her work, Strout has strong memories of his lab as a place where she was allowed to wander freely. "I remember the chemical smell of the building, and even now it makes me happy to remember," she says, "because my father, though a very distracted man, was always glad to see me." One sees in this glimpse of her father shades of the mild-mannered Henry Kitteridge, Olive's long-suffering husband, and one of the sweeter male characters to emerge in recent fiction.

Strout admits that "the bleak loneliness of Maine has influenced me profoundly," but goes on to confess that "I didn't want that to be the case, so it took many years for me to accept it." Although it is not unusual for a young writer to struggle to find her material, Strout took a unique approach to addressing the challenge by signing up for a stand-up comedy course in New York, where she has lived for over twenty years. She was terrified by the experience of standing before a crowd at a comedy club, but she realized that what got the most laughs were her stories about growing up in New England.

Strout has spoken at length in previous interviews about her life in New Hampshire and the self-imposed isolation of her family. When asked about her childhood, she elaborates, "I ended up spending hours alone with tree toads and pine needles, and turtles and creeks, and the coastline, and collecting periwinkles, so I think it is right to say that my interests when I was young were the beauties of the physical world."

Her early training both for solitude and for observation is apparent in all three of her books. The New England landscape is as much a character as the people. And her characters are often both leery of and hungry for human connection. In the relationship at the center of *Amy and Isabelle*, Isabelle, a single mother, seeks, through isolation and strict control, to protect her daughter Amy from the things that damaged her as a young woman: not allowing her to go out with friends, living outside the town. Her efforts fail, of course, and there is inevitably a fierce struggle as Amy begins to assert herself, first by defiance and then through deception. The novel is a compelling narrative about the futility of such attempts to protect those we love.

Strout has written about how her own parents were very strict while she was growing up. For her and her brother there was no television, no newspapers. No parties, no dates. As Bob Thompson concludes in a *Washington Post* article, it's "small wonder that within this enforced isolation…Strout's mother became her world." As Strout put it in a previously published essay, "My parents came from many generations of New Englanders, and they had a skeptical view of pleasure." She adds, "My parents were not just traditional; they were strict with a rigidity that made me believe the world was a dangerous place and vice lurked at the door to combat virtue."

Despite this sense of isolation, or perhaps in part because of it, she loathed high school. She hated it so much that her mother finally consented to let her leave school her junior year, after which she applied and was somehow admitted to Bates College. "I loved college," Strout says, "but I was not an especially good student. It never occurred to me to study, I'm afraid, except in classes about American playwrights and…my criminology classes." She was having too much fun with what she describes as her "wacky theater group" to pay attention to classes.

It was James Hepburn, chair of the English Department at Bates College, who first took her writing seriously and encouraged her to continue. He allowed her to take several independent study classes with him where "he just let me write and he would comment, and I would turn in another story, and he would comment…it was enormously helpful, his odd belief in me."

Despite her inattention to classes, Strout did well enough in college to be admitted to Syracuse University's law school, which she describes as a "kind of trauma," though "the classes themselves were fairly interesting." She eventually graduated from law school *cum laude*, but not until first dropping out and then reentering the program after witnessing the desolate lives of women who shopped at the department store where she worked in the interim. To support herself, both before and after law school, she cleaned houses, worked in an ice cream place, worked as a secretary and a department store clerk, did office work for lawyers, and waitressed, as well as played piano in bars. Although she went on to practice law for six miserable months in Syracuse, she admits to feeling like "an unspeakably bad, incompetent lawyer for Legal Services." She quickly discovered she was not adversarial and left the profession.

While in law school, Strout met her husband, still a practicing attorney. Together, they have one daughter, Zarina, now grown. "For many years," she says, "my entire writing schedule was around my daughter…she was a good baby, and when she napped I would write. Because she napped best when she was in the car, I often drove somewhere, had her fall asleep, and would turn the car off quietly. So for a couple years, my writing time was done in a car in some warehouse parking lot or on a street in New York. Quite honestly, this worked very well." She adds, "I think working around her schedule was good for me. It took away choice, and I don't do well with choice. There were very specific times when I could write, and so I did…Routine is essential. For years I would tell myself, three hours or three pages."

During her early years as a writer, when she was sending out her work, Daniel Menaker at *The New Yorker* became her mentor. "He rejected all my stories, but did so nicely, and with increasing encouragement to keep going. That was huge for me. I had the sense that he got what I was going for," Strout says. Years later, after struggling to find an agent for *Amy and Isabelle*, she reconnected with Menaker, then an editor at Random House, and he published the novel.

When asked about her writing habits, Strout says she likes to write first thing in the day: "There is something about the day not yet interfering that is helpful—a sense of wide quietness…I also sometimes write again late at night. I seem to frequently have a burst of energy just about the time the rest of the city is going to bed, and I might work for a few hours then." As for where she writes, she says, "I need to work in casual settings: at the kitchen table, on the couch, perhaps while riding the subway, sometimes in a coffee shop." She continues, "I write by hand for as long as I can before typing it up, and once I type it…I will cover it with penciled rewrites immediately. A freshly typed page makes me nervous. I am not an organized person, and I am happiest when I'm working with messiness, both on the page and in my immediate surroundings." She admits to liking a particular kind of notebook paper but says she'll write on anything. She feels the same way about pens, preferring how certain kinds (not a particular brand) feel, and "I love a freshly sharpened pencil; I am very happy when I have a freshly sharpened pencil."

Typically self-effacing, when asked to comment on how her career has changed since winning the Pulitzer, Strout says, "It has been wonderful…to see Olive get out there into the hands of people, many of whom seem to identify with her, or at least take her into their heart— or hate her, that's ok too…but my own little inner life of being Liz Strout hasn't changed."

As for what she's working on now, she says, "I think I don't dare say much about my new work except that hopefully part of it takes place in New York City. Apparently I have to live somewhere for twenty-five years before I can use that landscape."

AVOCATION

A *Plan B* essay by Antonya Nelson

First, you need a kitchen table. Round, oak, surrounded by at least six comfortable chairs with the option of an additional, less comfortable, four add-ons. This prop is the heart and hub of the house. The captain's chair is occupied by the patriarch. He complains whenever someone opens the refrigerator door and whacks the back of his chair.

Yet he will never sit anywhere else. "Eighty-four hundred square feet of space," he is famous for declaring. "And you all have to be right here."

"You all" is the dramatis personae, a large extended family and its fans; and "right here" is an old rambling house land-locked in the center of the country, deep in the winter, the warm kitchen respite. The yellow pine floor is worn where generations have trodden, pondered and stirred and rinsed and repeated. Daily, weekly, annually repeated. The patriarch will die; great-grandchildren he could never have imagined will be born. Twins. One of them looks exactly like him. She and her sister will sit in his captain's chair, two plushy butts wedged there at the table.

All household business is conducted at this table. From early breakfast to late night bridge playing, with doll-making and homework and crying sessions in between. Spilled milk dripping through the crack. Haircuts, nail polishing, splinter removal, gadget fixing. Chemistry equations penned on paper napkins. Drunken scandalous confessions, offered to the group; whispered gossip when the subject has excused herself. You might find a dog on this table, some day when he thinks nobody is home.

The people who set food on this table for those assembled around it are oftentimes the focus of the room's attention. You rest your eyes on their activity. You sit bemused over a glass of wine and watch them chop onions or knead bread dough or pestle something gritty in a mortar. They move among stations, combining, separating, sending up pungent plumes, swearing, spilling, sampling. The air smells of bacon. Fennel. Garlic. Cinnamon rolls. Smoke. The light fixtures are muzzy with ancient grease and dust and fur. The cast-iron Dutch ovens are in constant rotation, 10 quart, 12 quart, 14 quart. Everyone—every single one—knows how to clean them. Every new baby in the family is photographed naked in the largest, holding a raw carrot, cabbage leaf on its head.

One twin was in the pot; the other grasped the lid as if to seal her sister inside.

The plot has every day been the same, no matter the change-up in personnel: begin with coffee and cookbooks, consultations, lobbying, votes. Somebody needs solace, an indulgence, a treat. Someone is currently anemic, so all will suffer liver. When was fish last served? Spinach? A grocery list, a plan, a timetable as elaborate as a train schedule—because the meringue whitecaps on the skinny niece's favorite pie (banana custard) have to brown, and the piñons for the recently un-closeted cousin's basil pesto must roast, and the oldest brother's birthday beef needs braising, and the wine reducing. Not to mention the toddlers' bland lunch, and the vegetarians' pious rations. Also, appetizers. Shrimp, brie, wild salmon, Cheetos, hummus, rye crackers that remind everyone of the long-dead lascivious great-uncle. At the sink, somebody unskilled but dutiful peels potatoes. The martyred sister-in-law polishes silver. At the electric juicer, the eight-year-old delights in lime duty. Margaritas.

There are noise-canceling earmuffs that go with the blender. There are onion goggles, perforated cylindrical baking pans, little shower caps for the lemons. Microplane grater, meat mallet, melon baller. Cheesecloth. Trussing string. Salad spinner. Costco knives. Twelve separate attachments to the antique KitchenAid stand-up mixer: what *can't* that thing do?

Cooking apprenticeship begins early; aprons hang on the hook in the corner for every size and wardrobe palette, a stepstool for the children. For the high cupboards. Flour all over the floor. Eggshells in the batter. Biscuits smudged gray from overhandling. Fingerprints in the frosting.

A flaming pie.
A bloody roast.
Unleavened brick-like loaf.
Sabotaged gazpacho.

Pricey parmesan. A pound of butter. Bitter black walnuts. Heavy cream. Apples. Pink wine for the girl turning 21. Fresh sage.

The kitchen, and cooking, becomes the great equalizer. Meals are egalitarian affairs, democratic endeavors. In here gather the liberal and the not, the overeducated and the under-, the credentialed and the unemployed. Wage earners, neighbors, hangers-on, black sheep. The mentally retarded. The psychologists. The professors. White collar, blue collar, dropout. The graduate student. The alcoholics. The artists. The pensive. The loquacious. The sullen. The honorable. The thieves—of actual goods, of virtual ones. The in-laws, the outlaws, the felons, the philistines, the innocent, the hungry. Everybody is hungry.

They're hungry and they'd much rather eat than, say, read. Reading, like writing, is a solitary pursuit. Plus, a terrible spectator sport. And a writing life only annoys the friends and relations, who might feel some by-proxy pride when faced with the heft of a book, but more likely suf-fer collateral damage from investigating what that same book contains. They much prefer the short-order cook to the short-story author. They like you *way* better at the food processor than the word processor.

True, creating and serving and eating a meal makes for a tiresome tale. The stakes are…low. The plot is…familiar. The characters are… somewhat irrelevant. The conflict is…(wo)man v. ground beef. The setting is…disappointingly domestic. Moreover, it's almost always a happy ending, and everybody knows the great stories conclude miserably, with loose ends and sad lessons, unpredictability. In fact, everything that makes fiction great is what makes cooking disastrous. And vice versa.

You never want to hear the cook say "I had no idea how it was going to turn out. The ingredients just started doing things against my will."

Which is probably why cooking is a perfect second skill, the one that defuses, diffuses, dilutes, counteracts, cancels out, and forgives the first one of writing. Everybody loves the cook. And the reviews? In total, the reviews of a writer's writing could never equal this, delivered post-prandially one Christmas Eve: "If I were on death row," declared the earnest, eldest, sated brother, the new patriarch, grandfather to those twins, "*this* would be my last meal."

Antonya Nelson's most recent collection of stories is Nothing Right *(Bloomsbury, 2009). She has a novel forthcoming in the fall (Bound; Bloomsbury). She lives (and cooks) in Houston, Texas, Las Cruces, New Mexico, and Telluride, Colorado.*

Recommended Books and Writers

The Geometry of God, *by Uzma Aslam Khan:* Meeting with a young man torn between progressive and fundamentalist ideals, Zahoor, an elderly paleontologist, shows him the cupolas of the Great Mosque in Cordoba. It was built in a period, he argues, when Islam showed a different face to the world, a time when "faith meant devotion to multiple pleasures—mathematics, poetry, music, anatomy, calligraphy...The mosque in Cordoba reflects that vision. It could not be built today."

Set in Pakistan, Uzma Aslam Khan's novel is an eloquent rebuttal to its own character's claim about modern Islam's single-mindedness. Skipping across eras and registers of culture—and showing devotion to pleasures as diverse as Elvis Presley and the Mu'tazilites, Aflatoon (the Arabic name for Plato) and evolutionary biology—it is both an example of and an argument for the essential hybridity of every society. "A language is like a person or a whale," Mehwish, one of Zahoor's granddaughters, says, "it comes from something else...it is mixed not pure." In Pakistan, which literally means "land of the pure," this proves to be a dangerous sentiment for all the characters.

Mehwish mentions a whale in her list because Zahoor and a team of scientists are searching for the missing link between land mammals and the modern whale. Along with his other granddaughter Amal, he looks for fossils in the arid Potwar plateau, the site of the prehistoric sea of Tethys. On the day that the eight-year-old Amal stumbles upon a bone from a transitional whale, Mehwish, still an infant, is blinded after being left out in the fierce sun by a maid. For the rest of her adolescence, Amal will have to be her sister's eyes—"I developed the habit of looking down," Amal says, a tendency which will serve her well when hunting for fossils as an adult, the lone female on every expedition.

Fossil hunting, however, has become a dangerous hobby in Pakistan—the book begins in the early '80s, during the Zia dictatorship and the Soviet invasion of Afghanistan. The rising wave of fundamentalism makes Zahoor a marked man. In some ways, he enjoys the controversy.

During his lectures, he loves holding forth on philosophy and religion, as well as science, and this brings him to the notice of the Party of Creation, an Islamist group funded, ironically, with American dollars looking to combat Communism. The party leader's son, Noman, is sent to take notes on one of Zahoor's lectures, and he becomes entranced by both Zahoor and his two granddaughters. The false report Noman eventually gives of this lecture reverberates through the rest of the novel.

Amal, Mehwish, and Noman narrate the book in first-person chapters, passing the baton between them as the story proceeds. Months and years pass between sections: as Amal gets older, her sexuality increasingly isolates her from the male scientists who once included her in their circle; Mehwish develops her own curious way of classifying and interacting with the world; and Noman remains divided between his fundamentalist family and Zahoor's more inclusive and confusing view of life.

All three narrators have distinct and convincing voices, with one similarity: like many people who keep switching between languages—in this case Urdu, English, and some Punjabi—they have developed a tactile relationship with language, and a corresponding love of wordplay. The book is stuffed with puns, both regular and cross-linguistic. This style is sometimes charming—"promise kiss" for promiscuous, for example—but occasionally tiresome, especially during Mehwish's chapters. There is a hopelessly inadequate Urdu glossary in the back of the book, but then being lost is one of the pleasures of traveling.

The use of multiple narrators also becomes problematic as the characters grow older and more independent, because Zahoor's story is lost along the way. He gets put on trial for blasphemy and is in limbo for several years, but this trial is never dramatized, and there are only summaries of what he is going through, since the narrators rarely get to interact with him. New characters and tangential subplots are introduced—a hidden romance, a sexual assault—and the conclusion of the book strikes me as less focused than what came before.

Nonetheless, there are always treasures buried among the rocks: a sparkling phrase, an intriguing bit of history, and, at least for readers outside of Pakistan, the realization that the same conversations that take place in America—about science and religion, modernity and the past—are taking place everywhere, and that the apparently decisive actions of a government, or a few loud fanatics, always conceal a welter of conflicting opinions. Khan's sympathies clearly lie with Zahoor, with open questions instead of fixed answers, but she also dramatizes the costs of uncertainty. "The young Pakistani is a cultural freak," Noman's father says in a speech. "His religion is whimsy…A small wind pulls him." These winds pull at the narrators throughout the novel, but they produce joy and knowledge, as well as anxiety. Some certainty may be nice, the novel seems to argue, but look at all the life you would have to shut out. No Plato, no Elvis, no Ibn Rushd—it's too high a price to pay. —*Akshay Ahuja grew up in New Delhi and Bethesda, Maryland. His writing has appeared in* The Gettysburg Review, Guernica, *and* Barrelhouse, *among other publications. He lives in Boston and blogs, occasionally, at* The Occasional Review.

Restoration: Poems, *by Christina Pugh*: If restoration is, according to Nietzsche, an act of revenge, then Christina Pugh in her second book enacts vengeance that seems devoid of fear, primarily because the object of this vengeance remains a mystery, beyond narrative construction. Pugh's *Restoration: Poems* defies and resists, as well as exposes, our Pavlovian desires for the explicatory and the voyeuristic. This is a restoration "free of the x-ray's zoom," if by x-rays she means the fleshing out of telling. Instead, Pugh's *Restoration* sublimates revenge into a language that is the "densest vessel" for one's words, where one returns to a previous dwelling, over and over, until a lyric, a song, is what remains.

The book's three sections invoke Freud's interpretation of dreams, but only as a backdrop, a template for departure from exposure and certainty. The first section, "Dream Work," attempts a reconstruction of the poet's pathos and memories by stitching together reality and dream narratives, Plato and Beethoven (as well as dance arabesques), "into fractals" (seemingly infinite and chaotic small repeating patterns of structure and sound that accumulate into recognition of, or identification with, a larger mysterious symmetry, which is immediately felt by the reader, even when not understood in a traditional analytical sense). In that regard, the dream work here is the dream of a triumphant poem. The more poems one reads in this book, the more one rereads the poems; the more one embraces the pleasure and wisdom Pugh asks us to engage in. "Let's not ask how it was made– / this swan in a blue window, / swimming in snow. It's the word beneath / that moves me the most."

By the time Pugh reaches the second section of the book, "Case History," we are face to face with Freud's famous Dora. The poet's rewriting of a historical document is in solidarity with Dora against a "dim populace" that has "loosened / [one's] syntax" and a "doctor" who "pried each noun / from its casing." Pugh does not interrogate but discomposes the hierarchy of power and language, which in Freud's time was "conscious and unconscious" and later became "a double helix / necklaced as DNA." Pugh's language is most delightful as it "dervish[es]" into new usage and resistance, for what is sublimative restoration without resistance. In "Notes for Dora" she subverts the Freudian narrative authority into a beautiful absence all her own.

Still, one senses a fear of things becoming "public now / as a herd stopped / at a stone / wall." In the third section, "Restoration: the Senses," there is the clarity of one who is "trellising a fugue" and tracing "the branching / of [her] own questions" "with the dignity / of syntax spent." What remains, then, are acts of naming: a beetle in somersault, or a kite as a "flag of a private country" whose boy is "digging in / to steady the skyline, // falconing a shore's / weight in flutter," "testing the glass / of the built world." It is in this wondrous world that the poet informs us that what she wants to restore are "the particles / that formed us / before we met." Restoration springs from the imagination of description where one is engrossed in the cellularity of language without being alienated or mocked. Restoration is where "every noise in nature / is also necessarily / historical." But this is not a history that pays homage to the tyranny of linear time: "listen / to the temple / in the word, the sound / that convalesces–". Perhaps *Restoration* is also a celebration of the imagination, a praise of how art as beauty is sublime. —*Fady Joudah's translations of Mahmoud Darwish's lyric epics,* If I Were Another, *is available from Farrar, Straus & Giroux. His poetry collection,* The Earth in the Attic, *was a Yale Series of Younger Poets award recipient in 2007.*

The Art of Syntax: Rhythm of Thought, Rhythm of Song, *by Ellen Bryant Voigt*: Robert Frost advises that the surest way to reach a reader's heart is via the ear; Ellen Bryant Voigt, in her illuminating contribution to Graywolf's "The Art Of" series, maps out the cerebral pathways along the ear-to-heart journey. A gifted poet and teacher, Voigt has long been masterful at breaking down—and thus building up—the music and thinking in lyrical expression (see, too, an earlier volume of essays, *The Flexible Lyric*). It's a pleasure to reencounter her vigorous eye and intellect as she contemplates syntax, the order of words in a sentence: not merely the grist for utilitarian, discursive communication, but rather the expressive organization of sound and music that engenders an intelligent love of poetry. Highlighting common syntactical patterns and their musical arrangement, exploring how poetic lines interact with sentences, and illustrating how phrasing can balance or undermine meter, relax or propel pacing, and score unfolding narratives, Voigt reveals a detailed topography of conjoined music and meaning.

Tackling the intramural activities of line and syntax is particularly complex and far from the "singular" issue that the series précis suggests. One notes, too, that a heady sibling volume, *The Art of the Poetic Line*, from James Longenbach, adeptly covers similar ground. That said, the insight that these two fine poets bring to bear yields a delightfully geeky intellectual pleasure: we poets *enjoy* considering whether lines are end-stopped or end-paused, whether enjambments are annotated or parsed, dissonant or consonant. If these aren't your foremost pleasures, hang in there. Even within the targeted milieu of writers and teachers, Voigt's rigorous grammatical fidelity—dallying with plosive consonants and copulative verbs here, objective and dative cases there, a slight obsession with the altar of subject and predicate—runs the risk of stalling. It serves, however, to chaperone an inviting complex of references, including theories on language acquisition from Piaget and Chomsky, musicology via Robert Jourdain, and the close reading of various poems. Thus, the only caveat emptor: patient reading, echoing the care and precision of its author's work, is necessary. As with a good lyric, you'll need to return to this compact volume and revisit its compelling pleasures.

Thankfully, her analysis of "elaborate but comprehensible structures" is buoyed by her appetite for and acuity with language. In particular, her figurative gifts and keen juxtapositions keep this uber-*text*book lively. It's no easy task to make grammar appetizing, but Voigt finds the right seasoning. Whenever a specialized lexicon threatens to evoke the mind-glazing, post-lunch torpor of afternoon grammar lessons, Voigt finds a pithy image or figure to ground the writing: thus, when speaking of subject-verb-object placement within a vast genealogy of sentence types, she likens syntactical patterns to a train engine that might appear "almost anywhere in the sentence, pushing some of its boxcars and pulling others." Seminal moments like these—as when she notes that memorable rhythm is "muscular, not merely skeletal"—anchor ideas with fresh and tangible figures. And she's witty too, as when she parries Frost's dictum about free verse as tennis with the net down with Charles Wright's idea that free verse is actually "the high-wire act without the net," or notes how syllabic measure may number the "pieces of fruit in the bowl" yet "fails to distinguish grapes from bananas." Humor and candor nicely supplement her analysis.

At her best, Voigt takes us through a poem both intellectually and kinetically, as when she recalibrates the syntax of poems by Stanley Kunitz and D. H. Lawrence, showing us an original's patterned effects by revealing what different lineation *wouldn't* accomplish—a kind of demolition that highlights the integrity of an original structure. Thus Voigt gives us an original version of a Stanley Kunitz line,

> *If the heart were pure enough,*
> *but the heart is not pure*

and an altered version,

> *If the heart were pure enough, but the heart is not pure*

in order to show how the short, parsing line—contextualized in a "series of assertions, sometimes thorny, sometimes breezy, [with] moments of sly reversal and qualification"—works more effectively than if the poet had chunked "logical parentheticals alongside his conditionals," thereby canceling out "units of thought" and "undermining the authority of the voice."

Other highlights include an enlightening choreography of Shakespeare's Sonnet 29. Voigt clearly outlines the mounting power of the poem's dominant periodic sentence and reveals how the formal muscle of meter mainly serves to reinforce the sentence: Shakespeare "puts syntax in charge" and keeps the instrumental grid of meter more muted. Voigt then presents a valuable counterpoint of a poem, Philip Larkin's "The Trees," and shows how its accentual-syllabic music takes center stage, its more variable sentence sounds barely discernible, a "small ripple on the foregrounded formal surface." With the rhythms of song (line) and the rhythms of thought (syntax) working separately and simultaneously—as with the hands and feet in basketball, "both at their own task"—the potential yields are marvelously flexible, "the language ordinarily spoken by human beings...intensified by the echoes of more regular and regulated patterns of song."

With flexible approaches to music in mind, Voigt contemplates the relaxed accentual patterns of Elizabeth Bishop's "The Moose" and syllabics in Donald Justice's work, finding nuanced layers of thinking afforded by more complex syntactic variation. Supplying her own versions of Bishop's drafts, with boldface type to indicate omitted words and italics for handwritten insertions, Voigt shows how Bishop discovered her braided rhythms through drafts of "trial and error"—an important inclusion, lest Voigt's thorough analysis suggest a poet's fully conscious address of all issues syntactic *as* one composes. In addressing writerly intent, Voigt, with a wink and nudge, lauds the "sometimes instinctive, sometimes fretted over preferences" that poets make in both the heat of composition and the cooler reflections of revision, weddings of the "analytical...and the intuitive."

Voigt concludes with a timely comment about aesthetics, dismantling any fears about how a book with formality and structure at its core might jibe with current de rigueur tastes of asymmetry and variation. Citing Apollo and Dionysus as well-matched opponents, Voigt suggests that wherever we wager our poetic chips—on "pattern over variation, or energy over order, or, currently, fragmentation and disjunction over unity and coherence"—it remains that the best players will "petition both deities." Voigt's larger concerns with poetic evolution out of structural wellsprings allows for a variety of aesthetics as poets swim with, against, and inside the syntactical currents of English.

—*Michael Morse is a 2009-2010 fellow at the Fine Arts Work Center in Provincetown, Mass. and has published poems in* A Public Space, Agni, The Canary, Field, Ploughshares, *and* Tin House. *He teaches English at the Ethical Culture Fieldston School in New York.*

All That Work and Still No Boys, by *Kathryn Ma*: In *All That Work and Still No Boys*, Kathryn Ma's emotional precision sheds new light on the interworkings of families, particularly the lives of Chinese Americans living in northern California. Ma's greatest talent lies in accurately capturing the particular rhythms of familial dysfunction—the long-running tensions, the entrenched dynamics, the fragile spots that, when pressure is applied, can lead to collapse—and her powers are on marvelous display in this fine debut collection of stories.

The title story is Ma at her very best. She masterfully illuminates the dynamics between Barbara, her four siblings, and their mother, who needs a new kidney. Lawrence, Barbara's brother, is the best match, but their mother refuses to allow her only son to make the sacrifice: "[she] has no intention of letting him give her a kidney. She's made that perfectly clear to Barbara. She's got four daughters but only one Lawrence. She wants the girls to draw straws from the second-best broom in the house." As the story unfolds, the layers of connection and disconnection, of disappointment and betrayal, are rendered with terrific nuance; from Barbara's inability to break away from her family and forge a life of her own to the explosive tensions between the sisters, Ma creates a richly textured world of intelligence and heart.

Another standout is "Second Child," which tells the story of Daisy, a tour group leader working in China, and her encounter with a troublesome American family. The family's vacation is scheduled to culminate in a "reunion visit" to the orphanage that once housed their adopted daughter, a tradition Daisy dislikes: "It's fun to see your old home! Take lots of pictures! That's what she tells the girls. She puts them on their trains and airplanes and charter vans for the last leg of their tour. She has herded them in Beijing, at the Great Wall and the Forbidden City, and in Xian to see the archeological treasures…Chengdu is where her duties end. She doesn't go to the orphanages with them; they are met on the other end by local guides who know the right people, who can make the introductions to the orphanage directors, and though she wouldn't go, no matter how much they paid her, she wonders how much those local guides get tipped."

Daisy's reluctance to see the orphanages is fueled by her parents' abandonment of their first child, also a daughter, on the steps of a police station, leaving her to an uncertain fate in, one assumes, an orphanage. This is a secret Daisy has carried with her for years and one she ill-advisedly spills to Sam, the son of the wearisome American family. Throughout the tour, Sam keeps disappearing—sending Daisy and his parents into a whirlwind, first derailing the group's schedule and then ruining Daisy's plans to return home for her father's birthday—in an attempt to prevent his parents from continuing on to the orphanage for his adopted sister's "reunion visit"; his antics create a perfect storm for Daisy's long-repressed secrets and pains to spill out into the open.

As in "All That Work and Still No Boys," Ma explores the heartbreaking devaluing of the lives of girls and women, the fragile bonds between parents and children, and the enduring power of betrayal, but does so in a way that shows the reader these elements of the world through a strikingly different lens, so these preoccupations are not merely repeated but enriched and complicated.

Occasionally, Ma dips into well-worn thematic landscapes—the exploration of race in a town outside sixties-era Philadelphia in "For Sale By Owner," for example, moves into what feels like overly familiar territory—but the vast majority of her excellent debut collection is distinctive and graceful. *All That Work and Still No Boys* marks the arrival of a deeply compassionate and subtle writer, in possession of a keen sense of character and an impressive dexterity of language. The voices of Ma's characters linger with me still, and I'm already looking forward to what she'll write next. —*Laura van den Berg's first collection of stories,* What the World Will Look Like When All the Water Leaves Us *(Dzanc Books, 2009), was a 2009 Holiday pick for the Barnes & Noble "Discover Great New Writers" Program. She is currently the Emerging Writer Lecturer at Gettysburg College.*

EDITORS' SHELF

*Book Recommendations from
Our Advisory Editors*

Tess Gallagher recommends
The Secret Scripture by Sebastian
Barry: "Since I've been living
near Sligo and Strandhill in
Ireland where the novel takes
place, I found it fascinating to
see Irish history played out in
terms of what befell women who
did not capitulate to societal and
family pressures. The novel is
double narrated by 1) a very old
woman who was more or less
locked in and forgotten in an
asylum and 2) her doctor. Hard
to put down." (Viking)

Dan Wakefield recommends *The
Awakener: A Memoir of Kerouac
and the Fifties* by Helen Weaver:
"This is a beautifully done
memoir by one of Kerouac's New
York girlfriends, who is also a
prize-winning French translator.
Her memoir captures the era and
many of the principal writers in
it with affection, honesty and wit.
A real gem." (City Lights)

Tony Hoagland recommends
Revolver by Robyn Schiff: "Robyn
Schiff is a wild new maximalist
talent with a sociological bent,
who makes mobile poems out
of the sagas and textures of
American culture—the Colt
revolver, perfumes from Calvin
Klein, silverware, the H5N1 flu
virus. Her pleasure in diction
and loopy inclusiveness is
Marianne Moore-like, but her
choices of subject matter insert
a sneaky persistent counterpoint
of ethics and politics."
(University of Iowa Press)

Tony Hoagland also
recommends *Metropolitan Tang*
by Linda Bamber: "I'm hugely
(still) enjoying *Metropolitan
Tang*, the deft, New York School-
ish, heartfelt and witty poems
of Linda Bamber. Intellectually,
texturally, and emotionally—
there's no level on which these
poems don't delight me." (Black
Sparrow Books)

Richard Tillinghast
recommends *The Children's
Book* by A.S. Byatt: "Byatt won
the Booker Prize for her earlier
novel, *Possession*. The new one
also involves an imaginative
journey back into the Victorian
Age, and into the fascinating
period when the massive edifice
of Victorian England shifted,
once Queen Victoria died

in 1901 and her son Edward came to the throne for that brief prosperous period of glorious excess before the First World War brought the whole thing crashing down. For its atmosphere, picture the film version of *Howards End*. This was the glorious age of children's books, which were good enough to be read by grownups. Think *The Wind in the Willows*, and *The Railway Children* by E. Nesbit. Like the great Victorian novels that this book is modeled on, it is a massive book, and it has its longueurs. It may in the long run be better as intellectual history than as fiction. But I am enjoying it." (Knopf)

Lloyd Schwartz recommends *More Than I Want To* by Margo Lockwood: "It's been too long since Margo Lockwood's last book. Her new poems have the same unforced freshness and wise and touching observation of the world and herself that her poems had when I first started reading her 35 years ago. What a joy to read about rain falling on a blue umbrella 'like crickets that were falling asleep' or 'the rattle of forsythia/against the wavery 130-year-old panes.' Thanks to Boston's Pressed Wafer press for this lovely volume." (Pressed Wafer)

EDITORS' CORNER
New Books by Our Advisory Editors

Amy Bloom, *Where the God of Love Hangs Out,* fiction (Random House, January 2010)

Marilyn Hacker, *Names,* poems (W. W. Norton & Company, November 2009)

Edward Hirsch, *The Living Fire,* poems (Knopf, March 2010)

Tony Hoagland, *Unincorporated Persons in the Late Honda Dynasty,* poems (Graywolf, February 2010)

Maxine Kumin, *Where I Live: New & Selected Poems 1990-2010,* poems (W. W. Norton & Company, April 2010)

Heather McHugh, *Upgraded to Serious,* poems (Copper Canyon Press, November 2009)

Kevin Young, *The Art of Losing,* poems (Bloomsbury USA, March 2010)

Richard Bausch's *Something Is Out There, Stories* was published by Knopf in February 2010. His most recent book is the novel *Peace* (Vintage reprint, 2009). He lives in Memphis, Tennessee.

Amy Beeder is the author of *Burn the Field* (Carnegie Mellon University Press, 2006). Her poems have appeared or are forthcoming in *Poetry, The Kenyon Review, The Southern Review,* and *The Nation,* among other journals. She teaches poetry at the University of New Mexico.

Dan Bellm is a poet and translator living in San Francisco. His third book of poetry, *Practice* (Sixteen Rivers, 2008), won a California Book Award and was named one of the year's top ten poetry books by *The Virginia Quarterly Review.* He teaches literary translation online for New York University.

Justin Bigos lives in Swannanoa, North Carolina. This is his second appearance in *Ploughshares.*

Paula Bohince is the author of a poetry collection, *Incident at the Edge of Bayonet Woods* (Sarabande Books, 2008), and the recipient of a 2009 fellowship from the National Endowment for the Arts. Her poems appear in *The New Yorker, The Nation, The Hudson Review,* and elsewhere.

Cathy Smith Bowers' poems have appeared widely in publications, such as *The Atlantic Monthly, The Georgia Review,* and *Poetry.* Her four books include *The Candle I Hold Up to See You* (Iris Press, 2009). She teaches in the Queens University of Charlotte low-residency MFA program and at Wofford College.

Ha Kiet Chau is a writer of poetry and short stories. Chau has aspirations to write poetry reflecting truth, human emotion, and imagery through her own unique Asian voice and style. She is currently a graduate student studying creative writing with emphasis on poetry at San Francisco State University.

Bruce Cohen is director of the Counseling Program for Intercollegiate Athletes at the University of Connecticut. His poems have appeared in many literary periodicals, such as *The Georgia Review, Harvard Review, Poetry, The Southern Review,* and previously in *Ploughshares,* as well as being featured on Poetry Daily and Verse Daily. A recipient of an individual artist grant from the Connecticut Commission on Culture & Tourism, he has two collections of poems, *Swerve* (Black Lawrence Press, 2010) and *Disloyal Yo-Yo* (Dream Horse Press, 2009), which was awarded the 2007 Orphic Poetry Prize.

Michael Collier is the author of five books of poems, including *Dark Wild Realm* (Houghton Mifflin, 2006), his most recent collection. In 2009, he received an Award in Literature from the American Academy of Arts and Letters.

Lisa Cupolo has been a doctoring screenwriter at Paramount Pictures, as well as a literary publicist at HarperCollins, Toronto. Her articles and stories have appeared in *Narrative Magazine, The Toronto Star, ArtAsia Pacific* and many other publications. She is completing her first novel, titled *Two Elizabeths.*

Carol V. Davis was twice a Fulbright scholar in Russia. Her work has been read on NPR and on Radio Russia. She won the 2007 T. S. Eliot Prize for *Into the Arms of Pushkin: Poems of St. Petersburg* (Truman State University Press, 2007). She teaches at Santa Monica College in California.

Jehanne Dubrow is the author of three poetry collections, most recently *Stateside* (Northwestern University Press, 2010). Her work has appeared in *Poetry, New England Review,* and *Prairie Schooner.* She is an assistant professor in literature and creative writing at Washington College, on the Eastern Shore of Maryland.

Robert Farnsworth's third collection of poems, *Rumored Islands,* was released in 2010 by Harbor Mountain Press. He teaches at Bates College in Lewiston, Maine.

Stephen Gibson's two previous poetry collections are *Masaccio's Expulsion* (MARGIE/IntuiT House, 2008) and *Rorschach Art* (Red Hen Press, 2001). His third collection, *Frescoes,* won the 2009 Idaho Prize for Poetry and has recently been released by Lost Horse Press. Other new poems appear in *Field, Prairie Schooner, Margie,* and *New York Quarterly.*

Doreen Gildroy is the author of *The Little Field of Self* (University of Chicago Press, 2009), winner of the John C. Zacharis First Book Award from *Ploughshares* and *Human Love* (University of Chicago Press, 2005). Her poems have also appeared in *The American Poetry Review, Slate, TriQuarterly,* and elsewhere. She is currently writing a column for *APR* titled "Poetry and Mysticism." In 2009 she was a Visiting Writer at the Vermont Studio Center and a Robert Frost Fellow at the Bread Loaf Writers' Conference.

Mary Gordon's most recent book is *Reading Jesus* (Pantheon, 2009). She has received a Lila Wallace-Reader's Digest Writers' Award, a Guggenheim Fellowship, the 1997 O. Henry Award for Best Short Story, and the 2007 Story Prize for *The Stories of Mary Gordon.* She teaches at Barnard College and lives in New York City.

Amy Hempel is the author of four collections of stories. She has recently won the Ambassador Book Award for Best Fiction of the Year, the Rea Award for the Short Story and the PEN/ Malamud Award. She teaches at Harvard and Bennington.

Bob Hicok's sixth book, *Words for Empty and Words for Full,* published by Pitt, will be out in early 2010. *This Clumsy Living* (University of Pittsburgh Press, 2007) was awarded the Bobbitt Prize from the Library of Congress.

Edward Hirsch's new book is *The Living Fire: New and Selected Poems* (Knopf, 2010).

Carol Keeley's work has appeared in *The Antioch Review, Oxford Poetry, Playboy, New American Writing, Columbia Poetry Review, Chicago Reader,* and elsewhere. Her first novel, *Resolution,* is set in Chicago's jazz scene.

Marjorie Kemper died in Los Angeles November 12, 2009. She grew up in Louisiana and Texas; much of her work was set in the rural communities of the Deep South. Marjorie's short fiction appeared in *The Atlantic Monthly, Chattahoochee Review, Greensboro Review, New Orleans Review, River Styx,* and other magazines. Both *Southwest Review* and *The Sun*

nominated her for the Pushcart Prize this year.

David Kirby is the Robert O. Lawton Distinguished Professor of English at Florida State University and the author most recently of *Little Richard: The Birth of Rock 'n' Roll* (Continuum, 2009). For more information, see www.davidkirby.com.

Mark Kraushaar has new work appearing or forthcoming in *Michigan Quarterly Review, Missouri Review,* and *The Gettysburg Review,* and has been included in *The Best American Poetry,* as well as the Web site Poetry Daily. He has been a recipient of Poetry Northwest's Richard Hugo award and a full length collection, *Falling Brick Kills Local Man,* published by University of Wisconsin Press in 2009, is winner of the 2009 Felix Pollak Prize.

Dana Levin is the author of *In the Surgical Theatre* (Copper Canyon Press, 1999)and *Wedding Day* (Copper Canyon Press, 2005). Her new book, *Sky Burial,* will appear from Copper Canyon Press in spring 2011. Levin is the Russo Endowed Chair in Creative Writing at the University of New Mexico.

Bridget Lowe is a 2009 "Discovery"/Boston Review winner and recent graduate of Syracuse University's MFA program. Her poetry has appeared or is forthcoming in the publications *The New Republic, Boston Review, American Poetry Review,* and *Third Coast,* among others. She lives in St. Louis.

Jynne Dilling Martin's poetry has appeared in journals that include the *Kenyon Review, Boston Review, New England Review, TriQuarterly, Indiana Review, New Orleans Review,* and others. She was a finalist for the 2008 Ruth Lilly Prize, winner of the 2009 *Boston Review*/92ND Street Y "Discovery" Prize, and a fellow at Yaddo.

Michael Milburn teaches high school English in New Haven, Connecticut. His second book of poems, *Drive By Heart,* was published by Word Press in 2009.

James Thomas Miller's work has appeared in *The Antioch Review, storySouth,* and *Blackbird.* He is currently a PHD candidate at Georgia State University, where he's also the poetry editor of *New South.*

Roger Mitchell's latest book is *Lemon Peeled the Moment Before: New & Selected Poems, 1967-2008,* published by Ausable Press in 2008. He is now poetry editor for the e-zine Hamilton Stone Review.

Honor Moore is the author of three collections of poems, most recently, *Red Shoes* (W. W. Norton & Co., 2006). She edited *Poems from the Women's Movement*

(Library of America, 2009), which was a pick for Oprah's Summer Reading List (2009). Her recent memoir, *The Bishop's Daughter* (W. W. Norton & Co., 2009), now out in paperback, was a finalist for the National Book Critics Circle Award.

Scott Nadelson is the author of two story collections, *The Cantor's Daughter* (Hawthorne Books, 2006) and *Saving Stanley: The Brickman Stories* (Hawthorne Books, 2004). His work has recently appeared in *Glimmer Train, Alaska Quarterly Review, Post Road,* and *Puerto del Sol,* and his new collection, *Aftermath,* will be published by Hawthorne Books in spring 2011.

Amy Newman's most recent book is *fall* (Wesleyan, 2006). New work appears in *Narrative Magazine, The Kenyon Review, Hotel Amerika, Witness,* and elsewhere. She teaches at Northern Illinois University and is the editor of *Ancora Imparo,* the interdisciplinary journal of arts, process, and remnant.

D. Nurkse's ninth book, *The Border Kingdom,* was published by Knopf in 2008. Nurkse received a 2009 Literature Award from the American Academy of Arts and Letters.

Joyce Carol Oates is the author most recently of the novel *Little Bird of Heaven* (Ecco, 2009). She lives and teaches in Princeton, New Jersey. "Distance" was composed on-site in a sealed-window hotel room in Vegas in fall 2008.

Rebecca Okrent has written for the *New York Times* and *Boston Globe* magazines. Her poems have appeared in *Western Humanities Review, Marlboro Review,* and *Provincetown Arts.* Her first book, *Boys of My Youth,* will be released by Red Hen in 2011. She lives in New York and Wellfleet, Massachusetts, with her husband, Daniel Okrent.

Linda Pastan's new book of poems, *Traveling Light,* will be published by Norton in January 2011. She received the Ruth Lilly Prize in 2003 and from 1991 to 1995 was Poet Laureate of Maryland.

Beth Woodcome Platow has published poems in various literary magazines and received the 2003 Grolier Prize. She holds an MFA from Bennington College and lives in Salem, Massachusetts.

Katha Pollitt is living this year in Berlin. Her most recent books are *Learning to Drive* (2008), a collection of personal essays, and *The Mind-Body Problem* (2009), a collection of poems, both published by Random House.

Chelsea Rathburn's poems have appeared or are forthcoming in *The Atlantic, Poetry, Five Points,*

and *The New Republic.* She is the author of one collection, *The Shifting Line* (University of Evansville Press, 2005), and was the recipient of a 2009 fellowship in poetry from the National Endowment for the Arts. She lives in Atlanta.

Eric Rawson lives in Los Angeles. His new book is *The Hummingbird Hour* (WordTech, 2010).

Jay Rogoff's latest book of poems is *The Long Fault* (2008), from LSU Press, who will publish his book of dance poems, *The Code of Terpsichore,* in 2011. His chapbook of sonnets, *Twenty Danses Macabres,* winner of the Robert Watson Poetry Award, will appear this fall from Spring Garden Press.

Nicholas Samaras won The Yale Series of Younger Poets Award with his first book. Originally from Patmos, Greece, and Woburn, Massachusetts, he is currently living on borrowed time, the exact details of which are provided, word for word, in this featured poem. In the time left, he resides in West Nyack, New York, where he is hurriedly completing his next book of poetry and a memoir.

Austin Segrest was a 2008 Tennessee Williams scholar at the Sewanee Writers' Conference and winner of Iron Horse's 2009 Discovered Voices Prize. Former poetry editor of *New South*, he teaches writing and Latin at Georgia Southern University. His recent work appears in *The Yale Review, TriQuarterly, Blackbird, Passages North, River Styx*, and elsewhere.

Alan Shapiro's most recent book of poems, *Old War*, was published in 2008 by Houghton Mifflin. In 2011, Houghton Mifflin/Harcourt will publish his new book, *Night of the Republic*, and Algonquin Books will publish his novel, *Broadway Baby*.

Faith Shearin is the author of two books of poetry: *The Owl Question* (Utah State University Press, 2004), which won the 2002 May Swenson Award, and *The Empty House* (Word Press, 2008). She has received awards from the Barbara Deming Memorial Fund and the National Endowment for the Arts. Recent work appears in *Salamander, Atlanta Review*, and *North American Review*.

E. V. Slate's stories have appeared in *The* PEN/O. *Henry Prize Stories 2009, New England Review, Crazyhorse*, and *Best New American Voices 2005*. She lives in Singapore and Cambridge, Massachusetts, and is currently working on a novel.

Charlie Smith is the author of seven poetry books, including *Word Comix* (Norton 2009), and seven novels, including *Three*

Delays (Harper Perennial, 2010). He is the recipient of Levinson and Aga Khan prizes and has been published in *Poetry, Volt, New Republic*, and *Narrative*.

Kathryn Staley's stories have appeared in *The Quarterly, The Malahat Review*, and *Boulevard*. She has also published two books of nonfiction. A beekeeper on Long Island, she is training to become a Jungian psychoanalyst. She lives in New York City.

Jeffrey Thomson is the author of four books of poems, including *Birdwatching in Wartime* (Carnegie Mellon University Press, 2009). He has also published an anthology of emerging poets: *From the Fishouse: An Anthology of Poems that Sing, Rhyme, Resound, Syncopate, Alliterate, and Just Plain Sound Great* (Persea, 2009). His website is www.jeffreythomson.com.

GUEST EDITOR POLICY

Ploughshares is published three times a year: mixed issues of poetry and prose in the Spring and Winter and a prose issue in the Fall, with each guest-edited by a different writer of prominence. Guest editors are invited to solicit up to half of their issues, with the other half selected from unsolicited manuscripts screened for them by staff editors. This guest editor policy is designed to introduce readers to different literary circles and tastes, and to offer a fuller representation of the range and diversity of contemporary letters than would be possible with a single editorship. Yet, at the same time, we expect every issue to reflect our overall standards of literary excellence.

SUBMISSION POLICIES

Please note that our reading period has changed, effective June 2010. We welcome unsolicited manuscripts from June 1 to January 15 (postmark dates). All submissions sent from January 16 to May will be returned unread. Submit your work at any time during our reading period; if a manuscript is not timely for one issue, it will be considered for another. We do not recommend trying to target specific guest editors. Our backlog is unpredictable, and staff editors ultimately have the responsibility of determining for which editor a work is most appropriate. We accept submissions online. Please see our website (www.pshares.org) for more information and specific guidelines. Unsolicited work sent directly to a guest editor's home or office will be ignored and discarded; guest editors are formally instructed not to read such work. All mailed manuscripts and correspondence regarding submissions should be accompanied by a self-addressed, stamped envelope (s.a.s.e.). Manuscript copies will be recycled, not returned. No replies will be given by e-mail (exceptions are made for international submissions). Expect three to five months for a decision. We now receive well over a thousand manuscripts a month. Do not query us until five months have passed, and if you do, please write to us, including an s.a.s.e. and indicating the postmark date of submission. Simultaneous submissions are amenable as long as they are indicated as such and we are notified immediately upon acceptance elsewhere. We cannot accommodate revisions, changes of return address, or forgotten s.a.s.e.'s after the fact. We do not reprint previously published work. Translations are welcome if permission has been granted. We cannot be responsible for delay, loss, or damage. Payment is upon publication: $25/printed page, $50 minimum and $250 maximum per author, with two copies of the issue and a one-year subscription.

Dorothy Sargent Rosenberg
Annual Poetry Prizes, 2010

Prize winners for the 2009 competition, announced February 5, 2010

$5,000 prizes to Shannon Amidon, Brian Brodeur, Brieghan Gardner, K.A.Hays, Jennifer Key, David Krump, Dawn Lonsinger, Susan L. Miller, Miller Oberman, Rachel Richardson, Ali Shapiro, Jennifer K. Sweeney and Sarah Sweeney
$2,500 prizes to Lauren K. Alleyne, Scott Cameron, Victoria Chang, Catherine Chung, Weston Cutter, Julie Dunlop, Henrietta Goodman, Kimi Cunningham Grant, Nicholas Gulig, Alison Pelegrin, Anna Lena Phillips, Joshua Rivkin, Chad Sweeney, Natalie Haney Tilghman, Christine Tobin and Rhett Iseman Trull
$1,000 prizes to Corinne Adams, Jenn Blair, Paula Bohince, Traci Brimhall, Danielle Cadena Deulen, M. Ayodele Heath, Sadiqa Khan, L.S. McKee, Matthew Nienow, Nikoletta Nousiopoulos, Idra Novay, Jennifer Perrine, Leah Makuch Plath, Ursula Sagar and L.J. Sysko
There were also fifteen Honorable Mentions at $250 each.

Thank you to everyone who entered and congratulations to our winners

We now happily announce our 2010 competition

Prizes ranging from $1,000 up to as much as $25,000 will be awarded for the finest lyric poems celebrating the human spirit. The contest is open to all writers, published or unpublished, who will be under the age of 40 on November 6, 2010. Entries must be postmarked on or before the third Saturday in October (October 16, 2010). Only previously unpublished poems are eligible for prizes. Names of prize winners will be published on our website on February 5, 2011, together with a selection of the winning poems. Please visit our website www.DorothyPrizes.org for further information and to read poems by previous winners.

Checklist of Contest Guidelines
• Entries must be postmarked on or before October 16, 2010.
• Past winners may re-enter until their prizes total in excess of $25,000.
• All entrants must be under the age of 40 on November 6, 2010.
• Submissions must be original, previously unpublished, and in English: no translations, please.
• Each entrant may submit one to three separate poems.
• Only one of the poems may be more than thirty lines in length.
• Each poem must be printed on a separate sheet.
• Submit two copies of each entry with your name, address, phone number and email address clearly marked on each page of one copy only.
• Include an index card with your name, address, phone number and email address and the titles of each of your submitted poems.
• Include a $10 entry fee payable to the Dorothy Sargent Rosenberg Memorial Fund. (This fee is not required for entries mailed from outside the U.S.A.)
• Poems will not be returned. Include a stamped addressed envelope if you wish us to acknowledge receipt of your entry.

Mail entries to:
Dorothy Sargent Rosenberg Poetry Prizes, PO Box 2306, Orinda, California 94563.

"I love the fact that people outside Seattle and all across America will be reading my story."

—Hana Mohamed, student
John Marshall Alternative School, Seattle

826 National invites you to help us grow this country's next crop of young authors:

VOLUNTEER your time by tutoring students one-on-one at a local 826 writing center or in a classroom helping kids write and publish books.

DONATE funds and supplies. Have your employer match a donation to 826 National or a chapter in your area. See www.826national.org/donate.

BUY 826 student books, or pirate, time travel, superhero, spy, robot repair, or space travel supplies, and Bigfoot scouting goods in our stores!

826 National *826national.org* · 826 Valencia *826valencia.org* · 826LA *826la.org*
826NYC *826nyc.org* · 826CHI *826chi.org* · 826michigan *826michigan.org*
826 Seattle *826seattle.org* · 826 Boston *826boston.org* · 826DC *826dc.org*

826 National is a family of nonprofit organizations dedicated to helping students across the country, ages 6–18, with expository and creative writing. Through volunteer support, each of the 826 chapters provides after-school tutoring, class field trips, writing workshops, and in-schools programs—all free of charge. Find out more at www.826national.org.

HR HARVARD REVIEW

Issue 36
FICTION
NIC BROWN
ARIA BETH SLOSS
BARBARA HAMBY
SARAH A. STRICKLEY
ESSAYS
JOHN MATTHIAS
KATHRYN RHETT
RUTHANN ROBSON
POETRY
SHERMAN ALEXIE
TERRANCE HAYES
SONIA SANCHEZ

Issue 35
SPECIAL FEATURE:
NEW ZEALAND
PATRICIA GRACE
C.K. STEAD
IAN WEDDE
FICTION
CHARLES CONLEY
POETRY
JILL BIALOSKY

Issue 34
FICTION
ADAM BRAVER
KEVIN MOFFETT
ESSAYS
MICHAEL COHEN
JAMES MARCUS
POETRY
KATY LEDERER
GARRETT HONGO

Harvard Review publishes award winning poetry, fiction, essays, drama, graphics, and reviews. Work from Harvard Review has been honored in:

BEST AMERICAN POETRY
2002, 2006, 2008
BEST AMERICAN SHORT STORIES
2003, 2005
BEST AMERICAN ESSAYS
2003, 2004, 2009
BEST AMERICAN MYSTERY STORIES
2006
BEST NEW POETS
2008
PUSHCART PRIZE
2001, 2004

It is published twice yearly, in spring and autumn, and is available by subscription and from select bookstores.

Visit us online at:
http://hcl.harvard.edu/harvardreview

Issue 33
FICTION
ANNA SOLOMON
DAN POPE
ESSAYS
RICHARD GOODMAN
NINA DE GRAMONT
POETRY
DENISE DUHAMEL
ILYA KAMINSKY

Issue 32
FICTION
NAM LE
WILLIAM LYCHACK
ESSAYS
J. KATES
AKIKO BUSCH
POETRY
KATHRYN STARBUCK
RAY DI PALMA

Harvard Review, Lamont Library, Level 5, Harvard University
Cambridge, MA 02138 Ph: 617-495-9775 Fax: 617-496-3692

PLOUGHSHARES

Stories and poems for literary afficionados

Known for its compelling fiction and poetry, *Ploughshares* is widely regarded as one of America's most influential literary journals. Each issue is guest-edited by a different writer for a fresh, provocative slant—exploring personal visions, aesthetics, and literary circles—and contributors include both well-known and emerging writers. *Ploughshares* has become a premier proving ground for new talent, showcasing the early works of Sue Miller, Mona Simpson, Robert Pinsky, Tim O'Brien, and countless others. Past guest editors include Richard Ford, Derek Walcott, Tobias Wolff, Kathryn Harrison, and Lorrie Moore. This unique editorial format has made *Ploughshares* a dynamic anthology series—one that has established a tradition of quality and prescience. *Ploughshares* is published in April, August, and December, usually with a prose issue in the fall and mixed issues of poetry and fiction in the spring and winter. Inside each issue, you'll find not only great new stories and poems, but also a profile on the guest editor, book reviews, and miscellaneous notes about *Ploughshares*, its writers, and the literary world. Subscribe today.

Subscribe online at www.pshares.org.

- -

☐ Send me a one-year subscription for $30.
   I save $12 off the cover price (3 issues).

☐ Send me a two-year subscription for $50.
   I save $34 off the cover price (6 issues).

Start with: ☐ Spring ☐ Fall ☐ Winter

Name _____

Address _____

_____

E-mail _____

Mail with check to: Ploughshares • Emerson College
                120 Boylston St. • Boston, MA 02116

Add $12 per year for international postage ($10 for Canada).